Bad Religion

Also by Jaxon Grant

Crimes of the Heart

Crimes of the Heart 2: The Aftermath

Crimes of the Heart 3: The Resurrection

Bad Religion

A *BnTasty* Novella

JAXON GRANT

ISBN-13: 978-1499742169
ISBN-10: 1499742169

Bad Religion

1

Why did I take this bitch-ass nigga with me? What the fuck was I thinking? Thankfully, this five and a half hour trip was nearly over. I could smell the fresh beach water from my car. All of this for one day at the beach?

I glanced over to him, shook my head and rolled my eyes. *This faggot ass nigga.* He was looking out of the window, bobbing his head, lip-synching, to the sounds of hip-hop up-and-comer, August Alsina. I swear, I should have just gone straight back home to Savannah. Why am I in a relationship with him?

"Bryce," he looked over to me.

"What?" I cut.

Silas stared at me for a second. He rolled his eyes and replied, "What the fuck you got an attitude for?"

"What?" I repeated, raising my voice.

"Fuck it, don't even worry about it," he threw up his hands in frustration. I kept driving, turning the volume on the radio even louder.

Silas Ingram, a junior at Morehouse College, is my boyfriend...*I guess.* He was about 5'8" with dreads that reached down to the middle of his back. I loved pulling on that shit when I was fucking him. His plump ass is what initially attracted me to him. Nigga had an ass like a bitch. When I saw him in Lenox Mall, I knew I had to get up in that shit. Silas reminded me of singer, Trey Songz. He had the same skin color and bone structure. Often times when we were out in public, people would come up to him and ask if he was related to Trey. It's crazy, but he's used to it. They say everyone has a twin somewhere.

Coming from Atlanta, the easiest way to get to Panama City Beach was to go through Alabama. As we left the Alabama state line and crossed over the Florida border, Silas turned back to me. He turned down the volume and said, "What is your problem? I thought we were going to enjoy ourselves this weekend?"

"I don't have a problem," I glanced down at my gas needle. *Forty-four miles to empty.* I looked up and saw a gas station at the next exit.

"Damn, Bryce," he pouted. "I swear 'fore God, I just don't get you. Damn."

"Most people don't."

He sighed.

I pulled into the gas station and parked my cocaine white Dodge Charger at the pump. I looked at Silas and asked, "Do you want something out of here?"

"Some water."

"Ight," I got out of the car, closing the door behind me. As I walked away, I glanced down at the white rims on my car. I smiled. My shit was looking fresh as fuck.

I walked into the gas station and headed directly towards the restroom. I had to get this piss out of me. As I opened the restroom door, some white dude was walking away from the urinal. He didn't even stop to wash his hands. *Nasty ass muh'fucker.*

Reliving myself felt so good—felt like I was busting a phat ass nut. I swung my dick a few times to get rid of the excess piss. I put my dick back into my red basketball shorts and headed for the sink to wash my hands. I tried my best not to let the water touch my 14-karat gold, wrist bracelet.

I stared at the mirror and thought to myself, *Bryce Harkless, you look damn good.* My parents may not have been shit, but at least they made good-looking children. I loved the way my black wife beater hugged my muscular body. I also loved the attention niggas *and* bitches gave me. I stayed my ass in the gym for that reason alone. I mean some people work out to be healthy; I work out so I can look good naked.

I was right at 6'1" and weighed in around a buck eighty—give or take a few pounds. I had smooth, flawless brown skin and a beautiful dick to match. I loved wearing basketball shorts, just so niggas can check out my dick print. Shit was funny, catching a nigga—especially another masculine nigga—checking out my print. I kept a low Caesar cut, with deep, dark waves. I loved making niggas seasick. I ain't even gonna lie...I just love attention. My best friend calls me an attention whore.

I was royally pissed off when none of the major

schools I wanted to play basketball for wanted me. Reality slapped me in the face when I was forced to attend some small historically black university. I knew the chances of me making it to the NBA, playing for a historically black college and university (HBCU), was slim to none. I guess I thought I was better than what I really was. It is what it is. So, here I am—a third year student at Clark Atlanta University. All hate aside, coming to Clark Atlanta turned out to be one of the best decisions I've ever made. I met my best friend, Renzo, here at Clark. We both entered at the same time and we're on the basketball team. Renzo hailed from Chicago; his brother, CJ Wright, was a NBA superstar.

I snatched a few paper towels out of the machine and dried my hands. I used the light brown paper towels to grab the door handle. *I wasn't touching that filthy shit with my bare hands.* Once the door was opened, I threw the towels in the trash and headed back into the main part of the store.

I grabbed my dude...my nigga...a bottle of water. If it ain't Zephyrhills, his ass won't drink it. *Ole picky ass nigga.* I got a citrus cooler Gatorade for myself. As I approached the checkout counter, I reached down and grabbed a pack of the white chocolate Kit Kat. I had a love affair with that candy.

I placed the candy, juice and water on the counter. "Is that all, my friend?" the Middle Eastern cashier asked. I couldn't tell if he was a native of Iraq, Pakistan, Afghanistan or hell—Bangladesh. He was one of them muh'fuckers, though. Arabs is what we called them back home.

"Naw, umm, let me get umm—fifty at the white Charger."

He looked out the window, and said, in a high-pitched voice, "Fifty on pump two."

I glanced outside to make sure he had the correct pump. I looked at him, nodded my head and said, "Yeah."

Once he gave me my total, I swiped my debit card and entered my pin number, 0313.

"Do you need a bag, my friend?"

"Naw," I shook my head.

He handed me the receipt. I grabbed my shit and headed back outside. I walked over to my car and gave Silas the juice and snacks.

"Don't eat my fuckin' candy," I said.

"Don't nobody want that shit," he said, as I walked over to the pump.

While I filled my car up, I looked around. There were a couple of people filling up their cars, as well.

It was a beautiful March afternoon. The sky was nice. The sun was shining. It wasn't too hot, so that was a good thing. Spring was definitely in the air; I could smell the damn pollen. I finished up and got back in my car.

"Thank you," Silas smiled at me.

"Gimmie a kiss," I leaned over to him. He smiled, leaned over and kissed me. I didn't care who saw us. Despite our issues, this was *my* nigga. I put my seatbelt back on and pulled out.

Our weeklong, college spring break officially kicked off once classes were over, today. I definitely need the rest and relaxation. My basketball team lost in the second round of our conference tournament. When we got back from the Southern Intercollegiate Athletic Conference (SIAC) tourney in Birmingham, I knew I wasn't going to class for the rest of the week. I didn't go yesterday and I damn sure didn't go today. I would've left yesterday, but I had to wait on Silas. This nigga had a midterm that he couldn't miss. We left Atlanta four hours ago, and headed south for Panama City Beach.

That was the ideal location, because, tomorrow, I could drop him off at home. Silas is from Quincy, Florida, a town just west of the state capital, Tallahassee. Once I dropped him off, I could continue on to my hometown of Savannah, Georgia, to spend the week chilling out and relaxing with my crazy ass family.

Damn, I couldn't wait to see my auntie's crazy ass. I miss her like it ain't no tomorrow. I can't wait to laugh to see her and my cousin, Tacari, go at it.

My iPhone started to vibrate. I glanced down at it. Silas looked over to me. I ignored the call. *We* had nothing to talk about.

"Who was that?" he asked.

"Nobody important."

He mumbled something to himself. I shook my head and started to search through my iPod, hoping to find something to lift my mood. I landed on rapper, Lil Boosie's, 2007 hit song, Wipe Me Down. I turned up the volume to the max, leaned to the side, resting my body on the door, and pressed the gas pedal a little harder. I was trying my best to get my mind off my *real* issues.

When Trinidad James song, All Gold Everything, came on, Silas leaned over to me. He reached his hand over to my dick and said, "Let me suck it."

I glanced at him, then back to the road and said, "I'm driving."

"Bae, I wanna suck your dick...right now."

Hearing him say that made my dick rise.

"See," he continued. "Your shorts tenting up. You know you want me to do it."

"Yea, but I don't wanna die either, shawty."

"Slow down a lil and let me do it," he eased his hands into my basketball shorts, resting them on my pubic hair. I eased off the seat a little, so he could pull my basketball shorts down to my knees. If anyone rode past us and saw what he was doing, they would probably get my tag number and call the police.

Wait—what da fuck am I worried about them for? *Fuck them! Stop looking in my damn car and keep your eyes on the damn road!*

"Oh, fuck, nigga," I moaned, as he took me into his mouth. My eyes kept floating back between the road and Silas' head, bouncing on my dick. I wanted to pull over and fuck him in the back seat.

He eased inch-by-inch of my dick into his mouth, until he reached the base.

"Fuck!" I yelled, as he did some trick with his throat that tickled the head of my dick. I love it when he did that.

Shit got so good, I pressed the brakes suddenly, causing the driver behind me to blow his horn and pass.

Normally, I can just sit back and get my dick sucked for an hour without nutting, but I knew I had to make this quick, so I could focus on driving. This head was gonna get us both killed.

With my dick still in the back of his throat, he

started to move his head, faster and faster, like a well-oiled machine. As I felt my nut building, I placed my right hand on his head and gripped it as hard as I could.

As my nut erupted like a volcano, I screamed a bunch of profanities. With my eyes closed, I unintentionally, started to merge into the left lane, not knowing another car was riding in my blind side. When the driver blew their horn relentlessly, I snapped out of it. That moment of euphoria was over. I got back into my lane while Silas took a napkin and cleaned my dick. Like normal, he swallowed my babies like a champ. *This nigga is a straight freak.*

"You good?" he smiled.

"Yeah nigga," I smiled back. "I'm real good."

I glanced at the GPS. Forty-seven more miles to go until Panama City Beach.

Then, reality hit me again. I fucking hate this time of the year. All that shit started to flash before me. I will forever be tainted with those memories. Why did I have to see that shit? Why did that have to happen to my family?

Lord, just get me through the weekend. Please. Hell, you better...you fucked me up in the first damn place.

"You straight?" Silas asked.

Agitated, I said, "Yeah."

"Damn, what the fuck, Bryce?"

"Silas, just shut the fuck up, ight. Just shut the fuck up and leave me the hell alone. Damn!"

"You know what—fuck you, Bryce. I'm so sick of this shit. Fuck you!"

"Fuck you, too," I turned up the volume of the radio and accelerated the car to 95mph. The quicker I can drop his ass off, the better. Annoying ass bitch.

2

By the grace of God, we arrived in Panama safely. Even though I drove like a bat out of hell for most of the trip, I didn't get pulled over by the cops. The last thing I needed was another ticket. My auntie will kill me herself if her insurance rates rose any higher, because of my reckless driving.

I booked the same hotel I did last year when I came down here my best friend, Renzo. This shit was expensive, but it was right on the beach. The water down here on the Gulf of Mexico is beautiful. People are always talking about Daytona Beach, but fuck Daytona—Panama is the place to be.

When we got to the hotel, I realized that Silas still had an attitude. If I wanted to get in that ass tonight, I knew I needed to straighten this mess out. I damn sure didn't drive eight hours out of my way to go to Panama and then drop his ass off at home, and not get some ass in the process.

Turning on my charm, I parked the car and said, "C'mon, bae."

"So, now I'm your bae?" he cut.

I leaned over, kissed him and replied, "You're always my bae."

He smiled and shook his head. As he got out of the car, he said, "I swear something is wrong with you. Are you sure you're not bi-polar or something?"

"I'm not bi-polar," I grabbed my luggage.

"I know you better stop speeding before you get a ticket."

"I know how to drive my car."

"I'm just saying," he shrugged his shoulders, as we headed for the front door.

As we walked into the hotel lobby, I immediately noticed the desk attendant checking me out. I caught his eyes shoot down to my dick print. I grinned.

"Can I help you?" he asked, looking at me then over to Silas.

"Yeah, I'm here to check in."

"Last name?"

"Harkless," I replied.

He searched his computer, smiled and said, "Ok, I have you here." He turned to me. His eyes landed on my pecs. He slowly eased them up to my face. I smiled. Silas cleared his throat. I looked at the clerk's name badge. *Duke.*

"May I have your ID and the credit card used to book the room," Duke said.

I reached into my pocket and grabbed my wallet. I handed him the required items. He typed something on his computer, then turned around and headed for the printer.

When I saw his ass hugged in those khakis, instantly, my dick started to react. Duke was a sexy white boy with dirty blond hair. He had blue eyes and was about the same height and muscle build as Silas. He couldn't be any older than twenty-five. This white boy was sexy! He reminded me of the character, Zack Morris, from the 90's TV show, Saved by the Bell.

I turned and looked at Silas—his eyes were locked on me. I didn't know what to make of his blank stare. The last thing I needed was more fucking drama.

When Duke came back to the counter, he had me sign my name on some papers. I glanced back to Silas and he was typing a text. There was a spare business card laying on the counter. I grabbed it and quickly wrote down my name and number on the back. I slid it back to Duke with the other papers. He glanced up to me and smiled. I nodded my head.

"Here you go, Mr. Harkless," he handed me back my ID and credit card. "Will you need one or two room key cards?"

"Two," Silas cut, focusing his attention back to us.

With a smile still planted on his face, Duke swiped the cards on his terminal then placed them in a small manila envelope. Duke finished up by placing the manila envelope in my hands. "Please enjoy your stay. Check out is tomorrow, at eleven in the morning."

"Thank you."

Silas didn't say anything as we rode the elevator to our floor. When we got to the room, I opened the door and saw that we had a room facing the beach. I placed my luggage down, next to the king sized bed, and walked over to the window.

"This shit is beautiful," I said.

"I guess," Silas retorted.

I turned, looked at him and asked, "What's your issue?"

"Nothing," he plopped down on the bed.

I shrugged my shoulders and faced the water. Silas knows I'm not one to keep questioning you. My philosophy is that you'll talk when you get ready to do so.

My phone started to vibrate. I reached in my pocket and grabbed it. I sighed. *Why does he keep calling me? I'm not in Atlanta.* I ignored the call.

"What you wanna do tonight?" Silas asked. "We got about five or six hours before the sun starts to go down."

I walked over to him and said, "We can get something to eat and catch a movie or something later tonight. It's on you. It's whatever you want to do."

"Good, 'cause I'm hungry."

I laid down next to him and grabbed his arms, bringing him over to me. He got the hint and straddled me. I placed my arms around his body, inching down to his ass. He started to kiss me. I could feel his dick pressing against my stomach.

As I eased my hands into his boxers, he started to pull away.

"What's wrong?" I asked, as he got off me.

"I know what you're doing," he said.

"Yeah, I would like to make love to my baby," I stared at him.

"I ain't prepared," he said. "Besides, I gotta shit."

I chuckled, "Too much information."

"I'm serious. We can do that later. Let me clean myself up. I promise, I'll make sure you sleep good tonight."

I smiled.

Once he was in the bathroom, I opened my luggage and looked for something to wear for our night out on the town. While I searched for an outfit, my phone started to vibrate. I looked at it. I had a text message, but didn't recognize the number.

"Hey Bryce..." the message said.

"Who is this?" I sent back.

A few moments later, I received a message that said, "This is Duke. I just checked you in."

I grinned, then typed, "Oh yeah. Waddup?"

"I'm about to go on break, you wanna link up?"

I glanced at the bathroom door and exhaled. *That'll be real fucked up of me to do this while Silas is right here in the hotel. God, you know my heart. Can I make this work? I mean he did just suck me off in the car. Shit, fuck it. I don't give a fuck. A nigga is always down for some head.* I sent back, "Can you just suck me off right quick?"

"Yep. Meet me in room 1104 in five minutes."

"Bet."

I grabbed my charger out of my luggage and placed it in my pocket. I walked over to the bathroom door, knocked on it and said, "Damn, nigga. You're stinkin' it up, ain't you." I chuckled.

"Whatever, Bryce," he yelled back. "Don't act like your shit don't stink."

"It doesn't," I laughed. "But seriously, I'm bout to run downstairs. I left my charger in the car and I'm gonna try and find something to drink. I'm thirsty as fuck, bae."

"Ight, I'm gonna get in the shower in a sec."

"Ok, I'll be right back."

I left the room and headed to the elevator. I went down four floors and stopped on the eleventh floor. When I reached the room, I knocked. Duke immediately opened the door. He smiled as I entered.

"What's up, bro?" he said.

I looked around the room. I always checked out my surroundings when I was in a place I wasn't familiar with.

"What's wrong?" he asked.

"Nothing," I cleared my throat. I sat down on the bed.

"I'm surprised you gave me your number."

"Why is that?"

"Look at you," he said.

"What about me?"

"I didn't think you were gay. But the way that boy kept looking at me, made me wonder. Is that your boyfriend?"

"Yeah," I cautiously looked around. "Is someone gonna come in here?"

"No, we're safe here," he eased over to me. "When you walked in the lobby, your dick print was like just sitting there."

"Listen," I cut him off. "My boyfriend is gonna be calling for me in a second. Do you want the dick or what?"

"Fuck, yeah, bro," he slid to his knees.

"Good, 'cause it gotta be quick."

"No problem. I can handle that."

With my legs planted on the floor, I laid back across the bed. He slid my basketball shorts down to the floor and immediately took me in his mouth.

"Damn," I moaned. "Suck that dick!"

3

I wanted to fuck him so bad, but I knew I was playing with fire. I needed to get my ass back to the room. After I nutted all over his face, I grabbed a towel and wiped myself off. I then used the other side of the towel and cleaned up his face. Luckily, no semen got on his work shirt. That would have been embarrassing—a big ass cum stain where everyone could see.

I slipped my balling shorts back up and said, "I 'preciate that."

"It was my pleasure," he smiled. "I've got a few more minutes. If you want to fuck really quick, I'm down."

"As tempting as that sounds, I need to go." *I've already busted two nuts today, getting that third is going to take some time. And, time is not on my side.*

"How often are you in Panama?" he asked. "I would really like to experience the full thing."

"Not often. Listen, you've got my number. If you

are ever in Atlanta, hit me up."

"Will do," he said, as I left the room.

As I headed back towards the elevator, I bypassed two, petite white girls, with big ole' titties. One glanced down at my dick, looked up to me and smiled. I smiled back. I looked down at my dick and shook my head. That thing gets me in a lot of trouble.

I rode the elevator up to my floor. I stepped off and said, "Shit." I pressed the button to head back down to the main lobby. I needed to grab something to drink, to fulfill my little fib to Silas.

When I got back to the main lobby, I spotted a soda machine. As I walked over to it, I felt my phone vibrating in my pocket. When I saw it was Renzo calling, I smiled and quickly answered.

"What dey do, Renzo?"

"Nigga, y'all made it?"

"Yeah, we're here," I swiped my debit card into the soda machine. "My fault. I meant to give you a call to let you know we made it here, safely."

"Whatever, nigga."

"I'm serious, I forgot," I said, as my bottle of fruit punch came tumbling out. I opened it and immediately started to sip on it.

"When are you going to Savannah?"

"Tomorrow," I said, heading back to the elevator.

"So you drove all the way down to Panama for a day? You do know Savannah is in the opposite direction."

"I'm quite aware. Silas wanted to spend some time together." I pressed the elevator button to take me back up o my room.

"But you don't really even like him like that,"

Renzo said.

"It is what it is," I brushed him off. "When are you flying out to Chicago?"

"First thing in the morning."

"Ight. Well get at me," I said, waiting for the next available elevator.

"Ight. Be safe, nigga."

"No doubt," I hung up the phone, right as the elevator door opened.

When I got back to the hotel room, Silas was sitting on the bed with nothing but his swimming trunks on. He looked at me and shook his head.

"What?"

"How long does it take you to run downstairs to get your phone and get something to drink? I've shitted, showered and ironed my clothes for tonight."

"I was talking to Renzo, thank you very much!" I rolled my eyes.

"What's bothering you, Bryce? Whatever it is, it's all over your face."

"Nothing is bothering me. I'm cool," I lied.

He shook his head. "Did you get your charger?"

"Yep," I pulled it out of my pocket. "I thought I had packed it in my luggage, but I guess not."

"Umm, hmm."

"What?" I walked over and placed the charger in an empty outlet by the nightstand.

"Nothing," he nodded his head. "You gonna change your clothes?"

"For what? We're about to get in water."

I took off my basketball shorts and stepped out of my boxer briefs. I pulled my basketball shorts back up and said, "Is that better?"

He stood up and nodded his head. I balled up

my boxer briefs and placed them in an empty bag. I pulled off my wife beater and placed it in there, too. I looked at myself in the mirror. *Yeah, I was definitely gonna get some stares this afternoon.*

"Are you finished looking at yourself?"

I smiled and rushed over to Silas. I pressed my body against his, forcing him to back into the hotel door. When he couldn't go any further, I leaned over and started to place kisses on his neck. I seductively slid my tongue across his face, landing at his mouth. I pried his lips open with my tongue. He allowed me inside. We kissed passionately for a few moments. I lifted his legs, and he finished it off by wrapping them around my waist. My dick was hard as fuck; his was too. I forced my tongue back into his mouth, rubbing my hands through his dreads. I could feel Silas submitting himself to me.

"I love you," I whispered.

"I love you, too, Bryce."

He used his feet to ease my balling shorts down. I helped him out and pushed them down to my ankles.

"Hold on," he said, as I let him down. He stepped out of his blue and white swimming trunks. I used my strength and raised his body to where his ass was planted in my face. I spread his apple bottom cheeks a part and glided my tongue into his ass.

"Damn," he moaned, as he gripped my head like a madman. I hope no one was in the hallway, because they were about to get an earful.

I licked around his hole, causing Silas to go crazy. I just needed to get it wet enough so I could slide my dick inside. It's times like this, when going to the gym on a daily basis, comes into play. Everyone needs strength and stamina.

When I felt the juices from my mouth, slide down his ass, and drip onto my feet, I knew he was wet enough. I eased him back down to where his ass met my dick.

"I love you," I said again.

"I love you, too," he smiled.

With his back still pressed against the door, I spit on my rod and guided it into his ass. His body knew my dick, so it opened up, allowing me access, the moment pressure was applied.

As I sunk into him, he moaned. My eyes rolled into the back of my head. *Home, sweet home.*

I grinded, easing all ten, thick inches of my manhood inside of him. The deeper I swam, the lighter Silas's body felt.

I started to slide in and out of his warm cavity, causing him to moan louder. With his legs dangling against my arms, I leaned over and started to nibble on his nipples.

"Damn Bryce!" he yelled. "Fuck me, nigga! Damn, I love your crazy ass! Damn, fuck! Oh, my God! Don't stop!"

I moved my lips from his nipples to his mouth, and kissed him, all while I continued to slang my dick in and out of his ass. He put his hands on my head, encouraging me to continue kissing him.

My thrusts into his ass were causing his body to bang into the door. In an attempt to stop it, I lifted him off the door and moved him to the wall, directly next to it. I pinned him against the wall and picked up my pace. His arms were stretched out. His left hand gripped the white moulding of the entrance door; his right hand gripped the moulding of the bathroom door. The sight of my dick sliding in and out of his ass, was about to drive me insane. I glanced back up at Silas, and his eyes were in the back of his head.

I bit down on my bottom lip, as I tried my best to hold out a little longer. It was just feeling to damn good.

For easier access, I stretched and pinned his legs against the wall. As I looked down, the only thing I could see was his ass greeting my dick. I got as deep as I could, and started to gyrate my pelvic.

"Oh, shit," he moaned. "You gon' make me bust. Don't stop."

With all my dick planted inside of him, I continued to gyrate my pelvic in a counterclockwise motion. I could feel Silas' body tense up. His ass muscles gripped my dick even harder, which instantly put me on edge. I continued to grind into my baby. His breathing intensified. It was feeling so good to him, that he started to pant.

"Don't stop," he said. "Don't stop. I'm about to cum."

"Me, too," I whimpered. "I'm 'bout to nut, nigga."

Just as I said that, Silas screamed at the top of his lungs. He skeeted all over his chest. As he nutted, his ass muscles squeezed my dick so hard, I busted deep inside him on impact.

We stayed in the same position for a few moments, allowing our bodies to calm down. I took a few deep breaths and then kissed him, as I slid out of his ass. I eased his legs back to the floor.

Before I walked in the bathroom, I looked at him and mouthed, "I love you."

He smiled and replied, "I love you, too."

4

After our fuck session, we headed for the shower...and fucked again.

All that sex made a nigga hungry. Fuck hungry—I was starving! I needed to get some food in my system. I don't know why, but I had a taste for some pancakes—at 4:30 in the afternoon.

As I put on my jeans, I looked at Silas and said, "I gotta taste for IHOP." I slid on a form fitting plain black t-shirt. I put on my jeans and topped it off with my new, black Jordans.

"That's cool," he smiled.

"We can go to the beach when we get back."

I remembered passing an IHOP en route to the hotel. Luckily, it was just a few miles away.

When we got back into the main lobby, I saw Duke. He glanced at me and smiled. As we walked out of the revolving door, Silas said, "What the fuck he smiling at you like that for?"

"What?"

"Don't play dumb with me, ok."

"What are you talking about?"

"That white faggot at the front desk! Da fuck he smiling at you like that?"

"Doing his job," I sarcastically said. "He's supposed to be nice to people."

He didn't say anything else as we got in my Charger.

We arrived at IHOP and was immediately seated. Since we both knew what we wanted to eat, we placed our food order, when the waitress came over for our drink order.

I looked around the restaurant. It was about at half capacity. There were a lot of college students in here. Since Panama City wasn't a college town, I knew they were, more than likely, fellow spring breakers.

"A fruit punch for you," the big-boned, red-haired waitress, placed my drink down. "And a Sprite for you. I placed your orders, so your food should be out in a few minutes. If you need anything, in the mean time, just call me over. Again, my name is Jamie."

"Thank you," I said, as she hobbled away.

I stared at Silas' beauty. He was really sexy. I just don't think being in a relationship is for me. He's really a good dude, but he doesn't deserve the shit I put him through.

"What's on your mind?" he asked.

"Just thinking about something Renzo said," I lied.

"Speaking of Renzo—"

"What about him?" I cut Silas off.

"You don't believe me, but I'm telling you he is gay."

I shook my head, took a sip of my fruit punch and replied, "Renzo is not gay."

"Yes, he is, and he likes you."

"Boy, stop," I laughed. "Trust me, ain't nothing gay about Renzo."

"You just don't wanna believe it," Silas said. "I'm keeping my eye on him. He wants my man."

"You're delusional," I exhaled. "Renzo is straight."

"But you're gay."

"So, gay people and straight people can't be friends? C'mon, Silas, you're smarter than that."

"I'm just saying my gaydar goes off the charts when Renzo is around."

"Well, you need to get that gaydar fixed," I sipped on my drink. "Renzo is not a threat to you or anybody else's man. And, even if Renzo was gay, you don't trust me to be faithful to you?"

He didn't answer my question.

"Damn, that's how you feel?" I asked.

"Bryce, let's not play that game, ok. I know you, and you have wondering eyes."

"Just because I look doesn't mean I touch."

Silas nodded his head and changed the subject. As he started to talk about one of his professors, I thought back to the day Renzo found out about me.

It was the spring semester of our freshman year at Clark Atlanta. Renzo and I were roommates. When you live with someone, you learn their routine. I knew that Tuesdays were Renzo's long days; I didn't have shit to do on Tuesdays but go to basketball practice. Since Renzo is gone all day on Tuesdays, I took that as my time to fuck around with niggas.

This dude, JT, who lived a few doors down from us in the dorm, was a freshman wide receiver on the football team. We met each other on that gay hookup app, Jack'd. Since he was a bottom, shit was great. On top of that, he had a nice bubble butt, and he was sexy as fuck.

We hooked up a few times during the semester. This particular day, JT hit me up early that morning saying he wanted to slide thru and get some dick.

"Shit, I'll hit you up when Renzo is gone." I sent back to him via text message.

"Ight."

I pretended to be sleep while Renzo dressed for school. About five minutes after he left, I got up to brush my teeth, wash my face and shower. The moment I got back in the room, I hit JT up. A few minutes later, he was knocking on my door.

I placed some towels down on the bed—that nigga liked to slob on my dick. The first time we hooked up, my bed sheets were soaking wet because of that shit. It had kinda pissed me off, because I had just washed my sheets. Now, I'm used to it. I expect it. I like it when a nigga get nasty on my dick.

I slid off my basketball shorts and sat my naked ass on the bed. He immediately came out of his cotton sweat pants. He placed a magnum and a packet of lube next to me, on the bed. Within moments, he was sucking me off.

A nigga like me can lay back and receive head for hours without nutting. If I'm trying to bust a quick nut, I just let it go. But most times, I just lay back and enjoy the pleasure. Getting head is a recreational activity to me, so I like to enjoy it. That nigga loved sucking me off as much as I loved being sucked off. Since shit was starting to feel real good, I reached over and grabbed the remote to our music system. I turned it on to drown out the moans. Young Money's hit song, Every Girl, started to play.

About a half hour later, the room door burst open. Renzo was standing there, looking at us. JT scrambled to put his clothes back on. I slid back on my shorts.

"I thought you said he was in class," JT asked me, scared, upset and frightened.

"He's supposed to be," I looked at Renzo. *Why wasn't he in class?*

"Renzo, please don't say shit," JT begged. I could see tears forming in his eyes. "If this gets out, I'm toast! Please, Renzo. Please don't say anything. Oh, my God. Please, don't say anything. I'll give you whatever you want, just don't say nothing."

"I ain't gonna say shit," Renzo said. "You straight, bruh."

JT looked at me then as if he wanted to kill me, then rushed out of the room.

"Renzo, I can explain," I said, trying to remain calm on the outside, even though my heart was about to beat out of my chest.

"I'm pretty smart. There is no need to explain anything to me," he walked over to his bed.

I exhaled and ran my hands over my head.

"I'm serious," Renzo said. "Your secret is safe with me. I ain't tripping."

"Why aren't you upset?" I asked.

"I am upset. I'm upset at the fact that you couldn't tell me that you fuck niggas. We're supposed to be best friends. Despite that, I understand why you wouldn't say anything."

He sat down on the bed and continued, "Listen, a few years ago, one of my family members came out to me. I would die for that nigga. When he told our family he was gay, I wanted to hate him, but I couldn't. I learned that everyone has to live their own life. I'm not here to judge you. You do what you do and I do what I do. Who you have sex with is none of my concern. I'm serious, Bryce. I really don't care. You my nigga. We've been down for each other since we stepped on this campus. I won't tell anyone."

I sighed and said, "Thanks, man. No one knows about me, except for the niggas I've fucked around with. If my auntie found out, she'd probably disown me. You just don't know how hard this is, especially when I want to be straight. Why would God make me like this?"

"I don't know," he got in his bed.

"I thought you had class," I quizzed.

"I did. When I got to my first class, we found out the professor had canceled it for the day. Some family emergency or something, I don't know. Since I had another hour to spare before my next class, I stopped and grabbed something to eat. While I was eating, I decided I wasn't going to any of my classes today. I was gonna use this time to rest. That's why I came back to the room. But, then, of course, I walked in on you."

"Are you gay?" I asked Renzo.

"Hell fuck naw," he said, disgusted. "I like pussy, nigga. Been fucking since I was thirteen. You my nigga, but I don't like niggas like that. So, if you wanna keep this friendship, don't come at me with that bullshit."

I laughed and said, "Trust, you ain't the type of

nigga I fuck with."

"Good," he chuckled. "Now that that's out of the way, I'm going back to sleep. Wake me up when it's time for basketball practice."

I glanced at my phone to check the time.

"So, what do you think I should do?" Silas asked.

I looked up to him and said, "What?"

"What do you think I should do?"

"What should you do about what?" I asked, dumbfounded.

"Did you not hear anything I just said to you?" He was frustrated.

I saw the waitress bringing over our food. I looked at Silas and said, "Yeah, I heard you."

"Man, fuck you, Bryce," he sighed. "You're full of shit."

"I'm sorry."

"You're always sorry," he said, as we received our food. Before the waitress walked away, she asked, "Will this be on one ticket or two?"

"One," looked at her.

"Ok. Enjoy your meal," she smiled, and walked away.

"Yeah," I playfully said to Silas. "Enjoy your meal that I'm paying for."

"Fuck you."

5

I managed to calm Silas down at IHOP. I explained to him that I was in a deep thought about when Renzo found out I was gay. I let him know I didn't intentionally ignore him.

When we got back to the hotel, we both changed into our beach attire. I brushed my teeth again. Then, I waited for Silas to get ready while he spoke on the phone with his mom, for a few minutes. Things were really looking up. It seemed as if all the drama was behind us—at least for the moment. Still, in the back of my head, were my real issues. I was trying my best to act as if they didn't exist. That shit wasn't working.

Silas wore his blue and white swimming trunks; I adorned my red basketball shorts—without any boxer briefs. I liked free balling. Neither one of us had on a shirt.

As we walked throughout the crowded area, we were instantly the center of attention. There had to be at least 30,000 students occupying the beach. A lot of different schools were represented.

Each school that was present had a pole in the sand, with their school flag blowing in the wind. Instantly, I saw flags for Auburn University, the University of Cincinnati, University of Kentucky, Tulane and Mississippi State University. There were other school flags located along the nine miles of shoreline that made up Panama City Beach.

This sugary white, sandy beach was a sight to behold. I've never seen water this clear. It's like you can look straight through the water. Shit was amazing. This portion of the Gulf of Mexico was beautiful. The sand was so rich it felt like silk to my feet.

Even though I loved beaches and being around water, I wasn't one to really fuck with it. I wasn't a swimmer, so I damn sure wasn't about to play in that shit. Silas, on the other hand, handed me his shit and dived right in.

I continued walking, letting people check me out, until I found a lemonade station. While the server fixed my drink, I looked down the beach. A little ways down, a crowd was gathering around an outdoor concert stage.

"Here you go," he handed me my drink. I gave him the cash and said, "Thanks, bruh."

As I turned around to go back to Silas, I heard, "Hey, sexy."

When I looked, the same two white girls that I saw in the hotel were standing next to me. I smiled and said, "Y'all stalking me?"

I turned my head and saw Silas marching towards me. *Oh, Lord.*

"How long are you here for?" the blond with the bigger titties asked.

"I'm heading out tomorrow."

"Damn," she sighed.

"Why, what's wrong?"

"She—we—want to have sex with you," the other replied.

"Wow, just like that, huh?" I looked over my shoulder. Silas was getting closer.

"No need in beating around the bush, right?" the blond girl said. "We're in room 1113. We'll be there around nine and we'll be waiting for you."

I smiled and said, "Ight," as Silas reached me. He stared at the girls, looked at me and said, "Why didn't you get me one?"

"Because you were in the water, nigga," I said, as we turned and started to walk away.

"I swear you're so fucking selfish," Silas said.

I nodded my head and headed back to the lemonade stand. After I paid for Silas' drink, we started to walk towards the crowd.

I saw a group of about four black fags, bunched up together, against a tree, dick watching. I knew that's what they were doing, because one made it obvious and pointed at my dick. The others in the group started staring, too. One of the dudes I used to fuck with introduced me to that practice. He said that he and his friends would go to basketball courts just to watch niggas dick prints in their basketball shorts. He told me a lot of gay dudes do that for fun. He said it was equivalent to bird watching—hence the name *dick watching*.

We finally reached the massive crowd, right as some rock band was starting to play. The white folks were into the music, but the black dudes were trying to find their next fuck. I slipped on my drink as I observed the scene. There were groups of niggas standing together all over the beach. I saw all the stereotypes:

The *skinny punks* who hate on everyone else...just because; the *muscle bound college football players* who only fuck white girls, but are secretly getting fucked by other niggas; the *big boys* who nobody wants until you have nobody else in your phone to call...they'll be happy to suck your dick, anytime of the day or night, and break you off with some cash in the process; the *faggots* who the ultra masculine niggas slur on in public...but will let them suck their dick in private; the *sexy ass bottoms* who have their ass on display, hoping to get it in with one or two muscle bound, big-dick tops for the weekend; *big dick niggas* like me, who have no issues showing the dick off to the world...because we can; the *DL niggas* with sunglasses on, looking at other niggas...even though a group of sexy ass females are with standing with them, thinking that's their man; the *group of straight friends*...who everyone thinks is straight...but two of the friends are fucking each other on the low, and no one knows; the *drug dealing locals*, who just want to fuck a nigga that ain't from their area, while the baby mama is at work.

I shook my head. The world of niggas fucking niggas is something serious. This shit is real. No matter how much black females try to deny and ignore it, this shit is real. If all the conditions are correct, your man can be gotten, too. *If he already hasn't been got.*

I glanced over to Silas and he was looking at me, look at niggas.

"What?" I said.

He shook his head. I could see that he was starting to get frustrated.

I put my focus back on the music. White people know how to have a good time. I smiled as the white people jumped up and down, partying to the music.

"Really, Bryce? Really?"

"What? What's your issue?"

"I can't believe you right now."

"What are you talking about?"

"I see you looking at those punks," he said.

"Shawty, you tripping," I nodded my head. "I'm just observing the scene."

Before I knew it, some nigga with a phat ass had made his way in front of me. His shorts sagged off his ass, showing his black, Fruit of the Loom, boxer briefs. I glanced down at his phatty and grabbed my dick, in hopes that it would remain under control. He turned around and lifted his head, as if he was saying *what's up*. I lifted my head back.

Damn, shawty was sexy as fuck. He had to be about 5'7". He had a fresh, low cut. His teeth were straight and pearly white. He was clean-shaven with a nice, toned body. *Small waist, phat ass...definitely a plus in my book.*

"These white people loose as hell," he said, as he turned his body and looked at me

"Hell, yeah," I laughed.

He looked at Silas and lifted his head. Silas didn't do anything back.

Dude rolled his eyes and turned back to me. He asked, "What school you from?"

"Clark Atlanta."

"Oh, word?" he said, excited. "One time for the

HBCU's."

"What you know about that?"

"I graduated from Alcorn State," he said.

"That's in Mississippi, correct?"

"Yep. But now I'm in graduate school at Georgia State."

"That's what's up," I smiled.

"Hell, yeah, we're right there in Atlanta together." He glanced at my body and said, "I see you work out."

"I do what I do," I grinned.

We were interrupted when some dude walked over and said, "Errol, what you over here doing?"

The dude, who I now know as Errol said, "Gone somewhere, Kenny."

"Hey," Kenny extended his hand. "I'm Kenny, please forgive my friend. He doesn't have any sense."

I chuckled and said, "Naw, it's cool."

Silas cleared his throat.

"Kenny and I both got our undergraduate degrees from Alcorn State," Errol added. Errol looked at Kenny and said, "He's goes to Clark."

"Cool, cool." Kenny looked at Errol and said, "I'm about to go the room."

"Ight, I'll be up in a lil bit," Errol said, as Kenny walked away.

Errol looked back over to Silas, and then put his attention on me. He ran his eyes over my body, and then said, "Back to what we were saying, before Kenny interrupted us."

"What's up?"

"I was saying I can tell you work out," he looked at my dick.

"Oh, yeah," I grinned. "I hit the gym up."

"Shit, I'm trying to find a work out partner. Can I hit you up?"

"Yeah, do that," I said, exchanging numbers.

"Fa' sho'," he dapped me up and walked away.

When I turned around, Silas was storming away. I exhaled. I thought about just letting him be, but I knew that would only cause issues later. I wanted to get back up in that ass tonight. Reluctantly, I followed behind him. I tried my best not to make a scene, so I kept a distance between us.

"Silas, hold up," I yelled. He kept walking.

I followed him back into the hotel. As I walked in, he was getting on the elevator. The moment we reached our hotel room, he yelled, "You don't have any shame do you?"

"What the fuck is your problem, Silas?"

He yelled, "What the fuck is my problem? *You* are my fucking problem!"

"So, now I'm a problem?"

"Damn, Bryce, you gonna flirt with that fucking nigga and I'm standing right there next to you!"

"I was not flirting with him," I looked Silas in the eyes.

"Bryce, fuck you, man. I can't take this shit. That nigga lives in Atlanta. You gave him your number—"

"He said he wanted to work out. Hell, you can come if you want."

He walked into my face and yelled, "How dumb do you think I am? Do you think I was born yesterday, fuck nigga? You just made plans to *fuck* that punk ass nigga."

"I made plans to work out with him," I turned around and headed for the bed. "I swear you be trying to make drama between us."

"Did you fuck that cracker at the front desk, too?"

"What?" I jumped up.

"Bryce, I'm not stupid. I try to give you the benefit of the doubt. I see how people look at you. I see how you look back at them. That faggot ass cracker was flirting with yo' ass, and you flirted back."

"You tripping," I slammed my luggage back on the bed. I put back on my black t-shirt.

"So, what, he sucked you up in the car when you were going to get your charger? No, wait, did he get a room and you fucked him in there? Is that why it took you so long to get back, talking about you were talking to Renzo? Oh, yeah, and those two big-tittied Becky's, that was on the beach—you made plans to fuck them, too?"

"Silas, shut up," I said, upset. I put on my jeans, over my basketball shorts. I looked over to him and said, "You're really starting to piss me off with this bullshit."

As I put back on my Jordans, he continued, "What about that big ass whale that served us at IHOP. When you went to the bathroom, did you fuck her?"

I yelled, "Silas, shut the fuck up!" as I turned around and grabbed him at the neck. I backed him into the wall, and used my strength to lift him off the floor, at his neck. I continued, "I told your ass to shut the fuck up. You're really pissing me off with this bullshit. I don't wanna hear your bitch ass talk no fucking more. I swear 'fore God, I will leave your ass right here in Panama."

Realizing that he was struggling to breathe, I

released him. He grabbed his neck and stared at me. I pointed my finger in his face and said, "You keep fucking with me. Keep on fucking with me, nigga! What, you want me to go fuck everybody? Or is that your way of telling me you fucking all these niggas? You guilty, nigga? Is there something you want to tell me? Are you fucking your frat brothers, Silas? You keep accusing me of doing shit I ain't even do. The white boy from the front desk? Really, Silas? You know I ain't attracted to white people. I leave the room to get something to drink and grab my charger but, according to you, I snuck away to secretly fuck the hotel desk clerk. Do you see how fucking stupid you sound right now?"

I could see tears falling down his face.

"Oh, so now you wanna cry like a lil bitch?"

"Fuck you, Bryce!"

"You know what," I bit on my bottom lip. "I'm gonna leave this room before I do something that lands my ass in prison for a long time."

He wiped his face and said, "You threatening me, Bryce?"

I stared at Silas, grabbed my car keys and left the room. I don't have time for this foolishness.

6

Frustrated, I got in my car and drove around Panama City. I didn't know what to do. I knew if I stayed in that room, I was going to take all my frustrations out on Silas. He didn't deserve that shit. God deserved it. This was all God's fault. Everything was *his* fault. *Fuck you, God! Fuck you!*

I wanted to cry, but I am too much of a man to cry like a bitch. So, I withheld it. I haven't shed one tear since *that* day. Six years. I damn sure wasn't about to start now.

I wasted my gas, driving around Panama in an attempt to clear my mind. That shit didn't work. I stumbled across a dollar movie theater. I looked at the listings. Nothing really excited me. Hell, what else did I have to do—go back and fight with Silas?

I'm not violent. I've never been violent...especially after all the violence I've witness in my life. I'm a lover, not a fighter. I'm a

51

ladies man—well, in my case, a man's man. Silas just knows how to get to me. He knows which buttons to push and how far to go. I just can't deal with his accusations right now. I have more pressing shit to deal with.

I swear I hate this time of year. Every year for the rest of my life, I will be forced to deal with this mess. I will have to revisit this crap every second week in March, until the day I die. *Fuck God!*

I took a moment to collect myself. I looked at my reflection in my rearview mirror. *Ight Bryce, snap back into reality. Get it together, nigga.*

Stepping out of my car, I looked around the parking lot. There were a lot of cars here. Hell, it was a Friday. What better way to guarantee a night of good sex, than to take your lover—male or female—out for dinner and to the movies.

I felt strange walking up to the ticket booth. I was alone. There was no nigga—or bitch, for that matter—at my side. Who comes to the movies by themselves?

Since none of the movies excited me, I looked for the next available showing. *I guess I can do that movie.* I stepped up to the window.

"What'cha seein', suga'?"

Is this bitch serious?

I stared at the old country woman. I'm from Georgia, so I understand the south. I understand the deep, southern accent; but, damn, this is fucking crazy. Has this bumpkin ever been outside of Northern Florida? Has she no manners? Chewing tobacco and talking to customers? When was the last time she cut that hair? She had split ends all over that shit. Fucking hair was damn near covering her face.

That's why she kept pushing it behind her ears. Bitch probably got lice or some other ungodly shit in that muh'fucker. Face got more wrinkles than a load of clothes, fresh out of the damn dryer. Bitch just sloppy. Ugh. Fucking disgusting. I don't have nothing against big people, but damn...lay off the ribs and potato salad. Who in their right mind would fuck this fat, sloppy, nasty, white ass bitch? She looks like she's straight from one of those run down trailer parks. I can only imagine what that nasty ass trailer, she calls a home, looks like. She needs to go on Maury and get a damn makeover.

"Suga', you alright? You staring at me like I dun went and dunt something wrong?" She grabbed a cup and spat the unwanted tobacco juices it. "Pardon me," she smiled.

My stomach churned. *This bitch is serious.*

"So what's it gon' be?"

"Umm," I cleared my throat. "Just one ticket for the Hunger Games 2: Catching Fire."

"Alright," she clicked on the computer. "That'll be three dollars."

I'm shocked her old hillbilly ass can use a computer.

I reached in my pocket and grabbed my wallet. I pulled out my debit card and slid it under the small glass opening.

"Nope," she shook her head, as she pointed to a sign. "We only take cash. See, it's right there."

I glanced at the handwritten sign. *These country ass crackers couldn't at least type the damn notice? Can this day get any worse?*

I exhaled, looked over to her and replied, "Ma'am, this is 2014."

"I'm not a fucking idiot," she snapped. She slowly said, "I know what Goddamn year it is. The sign says cash only. While you're standing there judging me in your head, can you even fucking read?"

I leaned into the window and softly said, "Listen, bitch. I ain't in the fucking mood for your nasty ass attitude."

"Let me tell you something," she cleared her throat. "We don't like y'all Obama niggers 'round here. Now you bests to get, 'fore I go 'n call Billy. I don't care what fucking colored is in the White House, this is still the south. Now, you bets' to respect that."

I opened my wallet and grabbed three-one dollar bills. I slapped it on the counter. I looked her in the eyes and said, "What you gonna do, have Billy and company lynch me? Your rhetoric—if you even know what that word means—doesn't frighten me. I was born and raised in Georgia, ma'am. I've seen and heard worse. Hell, killing me might just take me out of my fucking misery, anyway. Now give me the damn ticket so I can watch the fucking movie. *Please*."

I forced a smile.

She rolled her eyes, took the money and placed the ticket on the counter. I snatched it up, smiled and mocked her deep southern accent when I said, "Now you have a good night suga', okay."

I nodded my head, as I walked in the theater. These crackers don't fucking scare me.

Nasty ass, fat ass, bitch.

7

I will admit, when the movie was over, I was cautious of my surroundings. As I walked out of the theater, I checked left and right, front and back, several times. The last thing I needed was someone ganging up on me. I didn't see the old hag at the ticket window, either.

When I reached my car, I exhaled. My stomach was growling a little bit. I knew I needed to grab something to eat. I checked the time—it was almost nine o'clock.

I sat in my car for a few minutes. I wanted to make sure I didn't see anything crazy. I didn't trust these country white people. Seeing that nothing was out of the ordinary, I backed out of the parking space and left the theater. During my ride to Wendy's, I looked in my rearview mirror several times, making sure no one was following me.

After I received my meal, I proceeded to eat and

drive. I finished up my spicy chicken sandwich and fries, just as I returned to the hotel. I sat in the car and downed the rest of my fruit punch. *Why did I come back here?* I really don't feel like getting into it with Silas. Luckily for me, this beach never closes.

I got out of my car and placed my trash in the garbage. I bypassed the entrance door to the hotel and headed behind it, to get to the beach.

Before I stepped on the sand, I took off my Jordans. I held the Jordans in my hands, and used my black socks for protection to my feet. There weren't many people out. I assume most of the college students were off in their hotels getting ready for the club scene.

I walked alongside the water, but not close enough to get wet. I lifted my black t-shirt and sat down on the sand. I looked up at the night sky. There was a full moon. I continued to roam the sky and spotted a shining star. I smiled. *I know that's you. Why did you leave me here?*

I exhaled.

I'm so tied of Silas and his bullshit. Why am I in a relationship? I don't need to be in a relationship.

My thoughts were interrupted by my vibrating phone. When I saw the name, I sighed. *Why does he keep calling me? That has to be like three times today.* I ignored the call. I'm not in Atlanta; therefore, we can't fuck. There's no need in answering the call.

Images from my fight with Silas flooded my mind. I can't believe I allowed him to push me to that point, again. This shit isn't healthy. I do like him...sometimes. Seriously, though, he's nothing more than a warm body to lay up with at night and instant ass when I need it. I just need to man up and cut this off when we get back to Atlanta. Yep. I'm gonna cut this off next week. I would do it sooner, but I'll let him enjoy the rest of his spring break.

I don't even know the amount of dudes I've slept with, while I've been in a *relationship* with Silas. That nigga drives me to cheat. Even when I was being faithful to him, he kept accusing me of sleeping around—so eventually, I did. I just never stopped.

Silas is a good dude, but he's so fucking bitchy. The one thing I hate more than anything is a nagging woman, but a nagging man takes the cake! I already have a mother; I don't need another in the form of a boyfriend. If he would just shut the fuck up sometimes, maybe we could be something serious. I guess a two-year relationship is something serious, though.

When I first met Silas, shit was good. We got along well. The sex was—damn. Maybe that's what trapped my ass...the sex.

We loved the same things. We liked the same movies. We laughed a lot. He was smart. He was sexy. He went to a different school. He had his own shit. He wanted for nothing. I was vibing with that. But the sex—the sex couldn't be topped. Silas was a straight freak. I loved the way his ass looked when I fucked him doggy style. That shit was so plump. So masculine. Damn.

The same thing that brought us together, is tearing us a part. You should never build a relationship because the sex was good. You have no real foundation and the shit is destined to fail.

That's exactly what's happening here. I'm getting tired of him, and the sex can't save us. After those fifteen or twenty minutes of pleasure are up, you're still forced to deal with the same shit that pissed you off in the first place. That person that you don't really like anymore is still there. That's how other niggas crept into the picture for me. This relationship was designed to fail from the jump. It should have been what is was—fucking. A fuck buddy. Friends with benefits. Nothing more, nothing less.

The truth is that I strung Silas along, because I was afraid to lose him. I was afraid to lose another important person from my life. Meeting Silas took my mind off my issues. He was an escape from the real world. I became dependent on him—not financially, but emotionally. Silas saved me from my demons. I felt safe with him. I felt secure. When I laid in the bed with him at night, I slept peacefully. The nightmares didn't return when he was around. The haunting memories went away. Now, it's not working anymore. He's no longer beneficial to me. The memories return, even when I lay in bed with him. The nightmares still appear, while I'm holding Silas close to my body.

My auntie says to trust in God. Put my faith in him. Fuck God!

"Fuck you, God!" I screamed. "Fuck you!"

You keep taking everything away from me. Everything I love, you take away. Why? Why, God? Why did you make me this way? You made me this way. You did this to me. Now, you want me to suffer for the rest of my life, too? Fuck you! I don't even know why I believed in a person I could never see in the first place. I stopped believing in Santa Claus. I stopped believing in the Easter Bunny. I stopped believing in all that childhood bullshit I was fed. What makes God any different? Why do people believe in something they can't see? Ain't nobody ever come back from the dead to tell me God really exists. People live their lives, based on a book of words from two-thousand years ago. Get the fuck out of here with that bullshit. God is supposed to be almighty. He's supposed to be this great person; but, instead, he's brought nothing but trouble in my life. Fuck you!

Let me get the hell out of here before I go insane.

I stood up and wiped the dirt off my ass. I reached down, grabbed my Jordans and headed back to the hotel. As I approached the lobby, I shook my head. It'll probably be best for me to find a cheap, local hotel to rest my head for the night. If I see Silas, I might take all this anger and frustration out on him...and he really isn't the issue. My issue is with God.

8

The alarm on my phone woke me up. I hit the disable button to shut it off. I squeezed my eyes, open and close, a few times. I exhaled. I looked around this sleazy motel room. If my aunt knew I slept here, she would have a fucking fit.

I was afraid of catching some disease, so I kept my clothes on and slept on top of the green and burgundy striped, hard ass bedspread. I probably would have came out better just sleeping in my car.

Since all of my personal shit—toothbrush, underwear, deodorant—was in the room with Silas, I slapped some water on my face to wash away the cold in my eyes, then left this bullshit ass room. I should have hit Duke up last night. Had I fucked him, he probably would've put me in a room for free. Oh well.

On the way to the hotel, I stopped by McDonald's. I know what Silas likes for breakfast, so I grabbed him a sausage and egg McMuffin meal. I got myself a bacon, egg and cheese meal, even though I couldn't eat that shit until I brushed my teeth. Morning breath and fresh food doesn't mix.

When I got to the hotel, I rushed up to the room. I couldn't dare let someone see me in the same clothes, two days in a row.

Before I slid the room key card into the door, I took a deep breath and exhaled. I didn't want any drama. I just wanted to drop him off at home, and for me, to get safely to Savannah.

I opened the door and walked in the room. He was sitting on the edge of the bed, watching TV.

"Good morning," I walked over to him and handed him the breakfast bag. "I know you're hungry so, please take it and eat."

"So you're coming here to bribe me with food?"

"Just eat the damn food, Silas, shit," I ranted. "I don't wanna hear you bitch this morning."

"Whatever, Bryce," he opened the bag.

"Listen, I'm gonna go and shower. Get everything ready so we can go. I'm ready to get out of this fucked up ass city, and get home to Savannah."

Sarcastically, he replied, "Whatever you say, daddy."

I rolled my eyes, grabbed my toiletry bag and headed into the bathroom.

* * * * *

I really needed that shower. Once I dried myself off, I wrapped the white towel around my waist and headed back into the main room. Silas looked at me, as I walked over to the bed. His eyes roamed down to my dick. While in the towel, I grabbed my sandwich out of the McDonald's bag and started to eat it.

He cleared his throat and said, "Thank you for the food."

I took a sip of my orange juice and replied, "No problem."

"I don't understand you," he said.

"What I do now?"

"You're so hateful, but loving at the same damn time. We argue and fight a lot, but at the end of the day, you always seem to make sure I'm ok. You always make sure I never go without. I've been with you going on two years and you're still a big ass question mark," Silas stood up. "I don't get you, Bryce."

I don't get myself.

He continued, "I googled your name last night. Bryce means—quick moving, alert. That's so you. You're always on the go and always watching what's going on around you. You move like a thief in the night. So smooth at everything you do. I don't know, Bryce. I just don't know."

I finished my orange juice and placed the remains in the small trashcan. I sat down on the edge of the bed and removed my towel. Silas looked over to me.

He shook his head and said, "Being with you is like playing with fire. Everything about you is tempting. You use your good looks to get what you want. Just how I'm looking at you right now— everything about you is tempting. My flesh is telling me to go sit on your dick. You know how to make me feel good. Look at you, looking so innocent. You look vulnerable. But, you play games, Bryce. You are a mastermind. I'm supposed to be mad at you, but when I look at you...your body...I just want to submit to you. You have this hold over me and I don't know how to let it go."

"Let's just forget about last night," I said.

"Why, so you can fuck me?" he turned around. "I'm worth more than just sex."

"I love you, Silas," I sincerely said.

"That game isn't working this morning," he sat back down on the bed.

"It's not a game. I'm just dealing with a lot," I stood up and walked over to him.

He looked at my dick. He glanced back to me and said, "Well, when are you gonna start talking to me, Bryce?"

I kneeled down and placed my head in his lap. I exhaled. "I need you, Silas."

"Why do you keep fucking doing this to me?" he cried. "I can't take this shit, Bryce. I can't take this from you. Every time I pull away, you pull me back in."

I looked up at him and said, "I'm sorry. I love you. I don't know why I do the shit I do. I don't know why I cause you stress. I don't know, Silas. I know you are a good person. I know you mean well. I know I love you. I mean that. In my own fucked up way, I love you, Silas." I laid my head back down.

He placed his hands on the side of my face.

I continued, "This is my first male relationship. I don't know what to do. I don't have a blueprint in front of me. I'm learning as I go. I'm just dealing with a lot—a lot of family shit. Everything is so frustrating."

"So, talk to me," he said. "I'm your lover. I'm your man. You can trust me, Bryce. Talk to me. What's going on?"

"I'd rather not talk about it."

"Whatever," he pushed me away and stood up. "Just put on your damn clothes so you can drop me off. You're full of shit, will say anything to get what you want. All of this is a fucking game to you. I'm just a fucking game to you. I'm not having sex with you, so cut the crap."

"Fuck you, man," I stood up and started to put on my black boxer briefs. "I'm trying to have a sincere moment with you and you just brush me off like I'm a piece of shit. You always think I have a fucking motive for everything. This is exactly why I don't tell your ass shit. You over analyze every Goddamn thing. I wasn't trying to fuck you. I did that shit yesterday. I was trying to have a moment with you. I was trying to let you into my world. I was trying to open myself up to tell you what happened in my life. Just like a fucking nigga. Get your shit so we can go!"

"Bryce, I'm sorry," he walked over to me and tried to touch me.

I put my hands up, backed away and said, "Don't fucking touch me, ight."

He watched as I stuffed everything back into my luggage. I grabbed a pair of my black basketball shorts and a black tank top. It was gonna take me an hour and half to get him home. Once I dropped him off, it was gonna take another five hours to get to home to Savannah. I had a six and a half our trip to embark on. Well, that's what my GPS says. I don't drive the speed limit, so I'll be home way before then. Regardless, I was gonna drive comfortable. I put back on my Jordans and double-checked the room to make sure I didn't forget anything. I snatched up my suitcase. I grabbed my phone charger out of the outlet.

"Bryce, I'm sorry."

"Fuck you!" I brushed past him and walked out of the room. I turned around and said, "Oh yeah, if you ain't at the car by time I finish checking out of the hotel, I'm going to assume you've made other arrangements to get your punk ass home!"

9

He was waiting for me at the car. When I saw him, I rolled my eyes. I never said anything. I just wanted to drop him off and be on my fucking way. *Bitch ass nigga.*

When I unlocked the doors, I placed my luggage in the trunk. He followed behind and placed his there as well. He got in the car and slammed the door.

"Don't be slamming my fucking doors!" I barked.

"Fuck you," he reached for his seatbelt.

"You keep on...I got something for yo' ass."

"Bryce, just take me home. Damn," he pouted. "I ain't in the mood for you this morning."

I put in my B.o.B mix, and turned the volume on the radio to the max. I just wanted to get him home and out of my damn car. I sped out of the parking lot as fast as I could, and subsequently, out of Panama City.

During the trip to Quincy, Florida, my phone started to vibrate. Initially, I thought it was my auntie checking to make sure I had gotten on the road. When I looked and saw the name, I exhaled. *Why does this nigga keep calling me?* I ignored the call.

"You fucking him, too?" Silas cut. Even though the music was loud, I heard exactly what he said.

"What?" I snapped.

"Fuck, nigga, you heard me," he reached over and turned down the radio.

I yelled, "Da fuck you touching my radio for?"

"Who da fuck is that, Bryce?" he said. "That's the third time you've ignored a call in front of me. You fucking that nigga?"

"Here you go with that bullshit again."

"Stop fucking diverting," he stared at me. "You fucking dat nigga? Who is it, Bryce? Who da fuck is that? It ain't Renzo 'cause you'll take his phone calls."

"See, look at you, always trying to start shit," I glanced at him before looking back at the road. "You be trying to get a reaction out of me."

"So where the fuck did you go last night?"

I tried my best to ignore him.

He yelled, "Where the fuck did you go? You went and fucked that nigga from the beach?"

"Silas, stop!"

"Answer my motherfucking question, then. You storm out of the fucking room last night, then come back this morning like nothing even happened. What fucking world do you live in? Sleeping it off is just supposed to make it better? Then gonna try and run that game on me this morning, laying your head in my lap, so you can get some ass?"

I put my finger in his face and said, "That's

exactly why I don't tell your ass shit now. I was being sincere with yo' ass. I was trying to open myself up to you and you think I'm running game so I can fuck. You ain't the only piece of ass I got. Remember that, nigga! Fuck niggas like you come and go; but, I love yo' ass and that's why I put up with yo' bitchiness. I'm at my limit, Silas. I'm almost there."

"You gonna turn this shit around on me? You gonna play the victim? You're at *your* limit? You just admitted to fucking other niggas, and this is my fault? I deal with all your bullshit and this is *my* fault? Seriously, Bryce? Then on top of that, you threatened my life?"

"I didn't threaten your life."

"Yes, the fuck you did!"

"Whatever, man," I brushed him off.

"So, who is it, Bryce? Who did you fuck last night? You didn't even fucking call me...no text, no nothing. Why? Where did you go? Which room did you end up in? Was it the nigga from the beach, or the two big-tittied white girls. Oh, no, wait...was it the white faggot from the front desk?"

Everything inside of me just wanted to punch the shit out of him. I wanted to unleash all of my anger on his face. Maybe then, he'll shut the hell up.

"So, you just gonna sit there like a lil bitch," he continued. "You just gonna ignore me? That's a bitch move, Bryce. You a bitch now? Huh, you bitch ass nigga?"

I swerved my car to the far right lane. When I got on the side of the road, I forced my car to an abrupt stop.

"Get the fuck out of my car!"

"What?" he said.

"Get the fuck out of my car!" I stared at him.

"I'm not getting out of this car," he answered. "You've lost your damn mind."

"Then, shut the fuck up, Silas. I'm not fucking playing with your ass. If you say one more muh'fuckin' thing, I'm putting your ass out. Real nigga shit. I don't give a fuck who you are. I'm not gonna sit here and let you talk to me like that. Shut the fuck up. I don't want to hear shit else out of your mouth. I'm not playing with you, Silas. Try me, nigga. Try me!"

I stared him in the eyes for a few moments. I exhaled and waited for a break in the traffic. I eased back into the traffic, instantly increasing my speed. I had to get him out of my car.

About twenty minutes had passed. He hadn't said another word. I was cruising. My GPS said we were about a half hour from his home. I glanced down at my car vitals. I needed to fill up again. I wasted most of my gas driving around last night when I was pissed off. *I can just fill up after I drop him off and I'll be straight for a few days.* That tank of gas should get me home and extra miles to drive around for a little bit.

"Goddamn!" I yelled, as I passed a state trooper, parked in the cut. Gut instinct was to smash on the brakes. I did it, but it was too late. He clocked my ass. I knew I was going above the speed limit. I could feel my body getting nervous. I looked in my rearview mirror and he was pulling out of his hiding spot with his red and blue strobe lights on. *This can't be happening.* He zoomed in behind me.

"I told your ass about that speeding," Silas added insult to injury.

"Silas, shut the hell up," I exhaled, as I moved to the side of the road.

When I came to a complete stop, I looked in my rearview mirror and waited for the officer to get out of his car. When the door opened, I was shocked to see a black woman. She had her hand on her gun, as she walked over to Silas' window. It was probably the safest place for her to be, with all the traffic coming past my door. *Damn, this chick was thick—in a good way.*

As she approached, I pressed the button to let the windows down. She had on the brown and black, Florida state trooper hat. She leaned her head slightly into the car, and said, "Good morning, gentleman."

"Good morning," Silas and I replied, simultaneously.

She looked at me and said, "You do know the speed limit in Florida is seventy miles per hour."

"Yes, ma'am," I stared at her.

"Do you know how fast you were going?"

"No, ma'am," I nodded my head.

"I clocked you in at eight-eighty miles per hour."

"I didn't even know I was going that fast," I lied. "I was just driving, not really paying attention. I guess I was in a groove."

She looked inside the car and asked, "Is this your car?"

"It's in my auntie's name, but it's my car. I make all the payments and stuff on it. I'm in college."

"What college?" she pried.

"Clark Atlanta University," I smiled. I pointed to Silas and said, "He goes to Morehouse."

"That's good. What are y'all doing over here?" she asked.

"We're on spring break. We stopped in Panama City last night to go to the beach. I was dropping him off at home in Quincy, then I was heading back home to Savannah."

"Ight, do you have your license, registration and proof of insurance?"

"Yes, ma'am," I reached into my wallet for my driver's license and insurance card. I motioned for Silas to get the registration out of the glove compartment.

When Silas handed her all the papers, she glanced at the insurance card and handed it back to me. She said, "Wait here, I'll be right back."

She seems nice; hopefully, she'll let my ass off. Yeah right. A state trooper's primary job is to give tickets. She isn't letting me off.

The tension in the car was thick. I looked at Silas and he was shaking his head. My auntie was going to kill me. I watched as cars continued to pass us by on Interstate-10. A few minutes later, I saw her getting out of her car. She walked back to Silas' window and said, "Mr. Harkless, you were going eighteen miles over the speed limit. The fines in this county increase drastically, every five miles. At fifteen miles over, it jumps another hundred plus dollars. Because you've been very respectful, and y'all are in college, I'm going to cut you some slack. You're still getting this ticket, but I'm only putting you down for fourteen miles over, versus eighteen miles over. At eighteen miles, your fine would have been three-hundred and sixty-four dollars. I got you down to two-hundred and forty-eight. You have thirty days to pay or contest in front of a judge. This county does offer extensions; so, if you can't pay within thirty days, please contact the numbers I've highlighted for you. I just need you to sign here," she handed me the form.

After I signed my name, she gave me my copy. She said, "Y'all young men drive safe and drive the speed limit. I've seen so many people lose their lives on these roadways because of careless driving. Be safe and get that education. I love seeing young black males making something of their lives. Y'all have a good day."

I looked at the ticket and exhaled. I placed it in the glove compartment and eased back into traffic.

"I told your ass to stop speeding, and you told me that you knew how to drive your car. Now, you've gotta come up with this money to pay that ticket. You don't fucking listen."

"Silas, please shut the fuck up. The last thing I need to hear is your nagging."

"So, how many dudes has it been?" he asked. "How many dudes have you cheated on me with? Do I know any of them?"

"Are you serious right now?" I glanced over to him.

"Do I look like I'm fucking playing with you?"

"Silas, let it go, man. Let it go!"

"No, I'm not going to let it go. He yelled, "Who did you fuck last night? Where did you go?"

"If I told you I went to a watch a movie by myself and got another hotel to rest my head, so I could calm down, you wouldn't believe me. So, what's the fucking point? What's the point, Silas?"

"The point is all you do is fucking lie. You find a way out of every damn thing. You never answer questions. You always find a way to divert from the situation at hand."

I pulled back on the side of the road.

He looked at me and said, "Why are you stopping? I'm almost home."

"Silas, I can't take this shit any more."

"What?" he cut.

"I can't take this no fucking more," I raised my voice. "You do more bitching than a bitch. You drive me fucking insane. The only thing yo' ass is good for is riding my fucking dick...and you don't even halfway do that shit good enough."

"You know what Bryce, I'm really rethinking this relationship. Since you don't—"

"How 'bout this," I cut him off. "It's over!"

"What?" he said, stunned. The look on his face was priceless.

"This relationship is over. I'm done. I'm done with it. I'm done with you. I'm done with this!"

"Bryce—"

"Silas, it's over. It's over! *It's over!*"

He didn't say anything.

I continued, "This shit is neither healthy for you nor me. I know I'm not perfect, I never claimed to be perfect. I know I've done you wrong. I've cheated on you. I've done a lot of bad shit. Despite it all, I love you, Silas. I really do. But this ain't gonna work. One of us is gonna end up dead. Now, because I'm not an asshole, and I care about your wellbeing, I'll drop you off at home...but this relationship is over. Don't contact me again. Lose my number. Act as if I never existed."

He didn't say anything else as I headed for his house. He looked out of the window for the rest of the trip. I know it was harsh, but it's for the best. We've broken up before, plenty of times, but we've always found our way back to each other. This time is different. I'm serious. I'm done with this. I need to figure me out.

When I arrived at his house, he turned and looked at me. I turned my head. I couldn't look at him. It hurt too badly.

"So, that's it?" he asked. "Two years just gone?"

"It's for the best."

"We've been down this road before, Bryce."

"It's different this time," I said.

"Sure, Bryce. I'll let you calm down and I'll call you in a couple of days."

"I'm done, Silas. I mean it this time."

Sarcastically, he said, "Ok, Bryce, whatever you say. I'll call you on Monday or Tuesday. Get some rest, nigga. I love you, too."

He stared at me for a second and nodded his head. "Drive the sped limit the rest of the way back. Send me a text when you make it, ight?"

"Silas, I'm not playing."

"Send me a text message when you get to Savannah."

"Sure."

"I would ask for a kiss, but my mom is probably looking out of the window. I love you, Bryce."

I stared at him.

"So you're not gonna reply?"

"I told you it was over," I said. "I can't take this anymore."

"Whatever, Bryce," he sighed. "I'll call you next week."

I watched him carry his luggage up the three concrete stairs. As he entered the old brick house, I exhaled.

I meant it this time—it's over!

Before I backed out of the driveway, I changed my iPod to the sounds of gospel singer, Donald Lawrence.

I needed to ease my mind. I needed spiritual guidance. When his song, Spiritual, came on, I smiled and backed out of the driveway. Finally, I can ride in peace.

In just about five hours, I'll be home in Savannah. I couldn't wait to have some of my auntie's cooking. Lord, please just get me there safely. *Please.*

10

I was pissed the fuck off. I should have been home. Because of some damn overturned tracker trailer on I-10, what should have been a five-hour trip from the time I dropped Silas off, ended up being an eight-hour trip. I've wasted my entire Saturday on the fucking interstate.

None of that mattered now. Finally, I was approaching the Savannah city limits. As I merged off I-95N, onto I-16E, my smile got bigger by the second. A nigga was home.

About ten minutes after passing downtown, I entered my neighborhood. It wasn't the best of neighborhoods, but it is what it is. This is home.

I eased through the streets until I saw my auntie's car parked in the driveway. I waited to make the left turn into the driveway, until a kid who was riding his bicycle passed me. I checked the time. It was pushing 7:35. The sun was setting.

I looked at the single level, three bedroom-one bath, green with white trimming, brick house. It wasn't much, but it was home. Auntie Whitley didn't play about her flowers. I can tell she's been out planting, since the winter is basically over. I remembered one time, I was cutting the yard and she beat my ass, because I cut one of her flowers. Those were the good old days. Life was different back then. I exhaled.

I got out of the car and popped open my trunk. As I retrieved my luggage out of the trunk, my phone started to vibrate. When I looked at it, I saw that my fuck buddy from Atlanta was calling, yet again. I thought about not answering the call, but I knew if I didn't tell him I wasn't in Atlanta, he was gonna keep bugging the fuck out of me. Just as I answered the call, he hung up. *I wasn't calling him back.*

I saw my next-door neighbor pulling into her driveway. I slammed my trunk. Ms. Hattie was an old, southern woman. She was born and raised in rural Fitzgerald, Georgia, until she moved to Savannah when she was twenty. She's been here ever since. Even though she had to be about seventy-something now, she still got around by herself. She didn't need anyone's help.

As long as I could remember, Ms. Hattie has been living in that little house. She used to clean them rich, white folks houses. She prepared dinner for them, and basically raised their children, too. She spent all day and night, raising those white kids. My auntie says, one of Ms. Hattie's old bosses still gives her work to do once a week...just to put some money in Ms. Hattie's pocket. My auntie says Ms. Hattie and her boss are now, more friends than anything. Every Wednesday after Ms. Hattie is finished cleaning that white woman house, they go to Cracker Barrel for lunch.

I was friends with a few of Ms. Hattie's grandsons that she raised. We were all in the same age group. Raising them white folk kids is probably why her own grandsons didn't turn out well. Two are in prison. One got killed in a robbery attempt gone bad. The youngest one still lived at home with her.

"Oh, my precious," she slowly said, getting out of the car. *Do all southern people talk slowly? Is it for dramatic effect? I hope I don't sound like that to other people.* "Is that you, Bryce? Is that really you?"

"Yes, ma'am," I smiled, walking over to her fence.

"Boy, you get more and more handsome, eury time I see you."

Every time. I chuckled and said, "You don't have to be so nice, Ms. Hattie."

"You look real good, son," she nodded her head. "How is the college turning out for you, baby?"

The college.

"When you gon' be grad'ating?" she asked.

Graduating. I smiled and said, "College is good. I still have a couple of years before I graduate."

"I tell ya' the Lord is good. You all in college, doing big thangs wit' ya' life. Eurbody at da' church, real proud of ya'."

Everybody.

"You still playing that basketball?"

That basketball. I smiled and replied, "Yes, ma'am."

"Good—good, good," she smiled. "You keep on doing good thangs."

Things.

"Now, you know, if you keep the Lord first in your life, all thangs is possible."

All things are possible. "Yes, ma'am."

"You got you a girlfriend up at the college?"

The college. I smiled and replied, "No, ma'am. I'm trying to focus on school and basketball, not girls."

"Good—good, good," she nodded her head. "The last thang you need is some babies running 'round here. I'm so proud of you, baby."

Somebody come save me. Ms. Hattie is the sweetest lady, but she doesn't know when to shut the hell up.

"I wish my grandsons would have turned out like you," she exhaled. "I tried my best to raise them boys to the bestest of my abilities. I told them wasn't nuthing in dem streets but trouble. Lord, Jesus."

In my peripheral vision, I saw my auntie's porch light flip on. A few seconds later, my auntie stepped on the porch and playfully yelled, "Ms. Hattie, you better leave my baby alone!"

Thank you, God! My auntie to the rescue.

Ms. Hattie laughed, raised her hand and said, "Whitley, gurl, you know how I am when I see my Bryce." She hung her head and continued to laugh. "You knows I'm so proud of him."

"Yeah, I know Ms. Hattie," my auntie said. "We're all proud of him."

"Let me gon' in this house," Ms. Hattie said. "Y'all know I can talk fa' days. Let me gon' 'n warm up some of these collards, I made the other day. I think I got some more neck bones in there, too. I see y'all in church in the morning, right?"

"Yes, ma'am," my auntie replied.

"Good—good, good," Ms. Hattie smiled. She looked at me and said, "When you going back to the college, baby?"

The college. "Ummm, I'll be here all week. I'll probably head back next weekend."

"That's good. "I gots to make sure I whip up one of my pound cakes and red velvet cakes, so you can take back to the college."

That made me grin like a child on Christmas. "Yes, ma'am. I'd like that."

"Good. You know I loves to cook."

"Ms. Hattie, gon' in that house, now," my auntie yelled.

"Yeah, chile, let me go 'fore these 'squitas start bitin'."

Mosquitoes. I nodded my head.

"Don't it seem like they get bigger and bigger eury year," Ms. Hattie questioned, to no one in particular.

"Good night, Ms. Hattie," my auntie said.

"Good night," she smiled, as she turned around and headed inside her house.

When I reached my auntie, she extended her arms and pulled me in for a huge hug.

"I missed you so much," she released me.

"I missed you, too, auntie." I grabbed my luggage and followed her in the house. I went directly to my room and placed my bags down.

"Bryce!" she yelled from the kitchen.

"Yes, ma'am?" I closed my door and headed to her. When I reached her, she was sitting at the kitchen table, cutting up some collard greens.

"Grab me a glass of water, please."

She called me in here to get some water? Yep,

I'm definitely back home. Whatever.

As I fixed her a glass, she said, "What took you so long to get here? I thought you said you'd be here 'round four or five."

"Got stuck in traffic," I dropped two cubes of ice into the glass. "Some tractor was overturned and that held me up."

"That's horrible," she said, as I handed her the glass. She took a sip, and then placed the glass on the table. "I hope everyone is ok."

I sat down across from her.

Auntie Whitley was a mess. Literally. She was just as ghetto and hood as she wanted to be. She meant well, though. She's been through more men than all of the Kardashian's combined. Auntie was a long, slender, petite woman. She kept her hair and finger nails done, religiously.

"What you wanna do for your birthday?" I asked. "You'll be forty-nine this year."

"Don't remind me," she nodded her head. "Where has the time gone?"

I chuckled.

"Baby, look in that cabinet and see if I got some Jiffy mix up there. I need that for my Sunday dinner, tomorrow."

"No, ma'am," I nodded my head, looking in the cabinet.

"Any sugar?"

"Just a lil bit," I looked at the Great Value brand of sugar.

"That Goddamn Tacari, eating up all my damn food and not replacing my shit. I'm 'bout to kick that nigga out. You better talk to your cousin."

"I can run to the corner store and get it for you."

"Thank you, baby. I got a twenty dollar bill on

the side of my purse."

I walked in her room and it smelt like nothing but cigarettes. I looked on the side of her purse and grabbed the twenty. When I got back in the kitchen, she was writing something on a sheet of paper. She looked at me and said, "When you go to the store, get four quick picks and play these numbers for me. They got a nice jackpot tonight." She handed me the numbers.

"You still playing the lotto, auntie?"

"Hell, yeah," she said. "You can't win if you don't play."

I laughed and said, "I'll be back in a second."

11

While I was out fetching my aunt her lotto tickets, cornbread mix and sugar, I stopped by Popeye's and grabbed a two-piece chicken dinner. I called and asked her if she wanted something, but she said she was good.

On the ride home, I thought about Silas. Just so he could sleep better tonight, I sent him a text letting him know I made it to Savannah.

Instantly, he replied, "Thank you for letting me know. We'll work out our issues when we get back to Atlanta."

I didn't reply to his message. I'm serious. I'm done with this relationship shit.

When I got back in the house, I placed the food up in the cabinet. I handed my aunt her lotto tickets and her change. I sat down at the table and opened my Popeye's box.

Just as she was getting ready to speak, her house phone stared to ring. It must have been one of her girlfriends, because she instantly got into gossip mode.

I exhaled and ate my chicken in peace. After I finished my food, she hung up the phone. She looked at me and said, "That was Mary. She told me to tell you hey, and you better come see her while you're home."

"Ok," I said. Mary was my aunt's best friend.

"What you got planned for the evening?" she asked.

"Nothing, really."

"Well, I'm just letting you know—you getting ya' ass up and coming to church with me in the morning."

"Auntie, I'm tired," I said. "I've been driving all day."

"Well, get ya' ass in the bed. I ain't tell you to take ya' ass to Panama City. Ain't shit changed 'round here. You can give the Lord a few hours of your time."

Fuck the Lord.

"The last time ya' ass probably went to church is when you were here during Christmas, two years ago." she said. "I know you ain't going to church up there in Atlanta. If the Lord treated us the way the way we treat him—"

"Where is Tacari?" I cut her off. I didn't want to hear that bullshit.

"He's at work. He'll be home later."

"Well, I'm gonna go relax for a lil bit," I kissed her on the cheek, before placing the Popeye's box in the garbage.

"Ight, now, set that clock," she said, as I hurried off to my room. She yelled, "We're leaving at 10:30 in the morning!"

I sat down on my childhood bed, and exhaled. I grabbed my arms, as goosebumps overcame my body.

I scooted up to the head of the bed and laid down. I looked to my left and stared at my nightstand.

I grabbed the old family picture of my mom, stepdad, older brother, Russell, and me. We all looked so happy back then. I couldn't have been any older than four years old.

I never knew or met my biological father, even though I carried his last name, Harkless. The man I knew to act as my dad was named, Fred. My mom, Josephine, was in love with him. I was five when everything in my life started to change.

My mom and stepdad had been arguing for a few days, although I can't remember what it was about. I remembered being scared. I remembered my brother, Russell, protecting me and hiding me in the closet. Russell was two years older than I was. Even though we hid, we still heard the arguing and fighting.

This night in question was the worst. We couldn't sleep. They wouldn't shut up. When I got out of the bed to use the bathroom, I walked in the living room to see what exactly they were doing. I watched my stepdad put a gun to his head. I watched him pull the trigger. I watched pieces of his brain explode from his head. I watched his blood splatter over my mother and onto the wall. I watched his limp body fall to the ground. I could still hear her scream. It rings in my head. I was five.

That event changed my mother. I watched her deteriorate. I watched her depend on drugs for support. Before long, she was a goner. She was strung out on drugs. My family tried everything to try and fix her, but she didn't want to be fixed.

While my mother battled her drug issues, my grandmother took Russell and me into her home. She tried her best to make our lives as normal as possible. Then, she left. I was eight when my grandmother went to sleep and never woke up.

Insert Aunt Whitley. She was my mom's older sister. When my grandma died, Aunt Whitley made room in her house for two more boys. She already had two children of her own. When we moved with Aunt Whitley, her oldest, my cousin Alexis—everyone just calls her Lexi—left a year later to go to Florida A&M University (FAMU) for college. She's like ten years older than I am.

Her other son, Tacari—who is three years older than me, and a year older than Russell—became like a brother to us. Tacari, Russell and Bryce. We couldn't be separated. Since I was the youngest, Tacari and Russell made sure they protected me from all hurt, harm and danger.

Auntie Whitley tried her best to get Russell and me to talk to our mother. Neither one of us was having that shit. The last time I saw my mother was at my grandmother's funeral. If it weren't for my auntie, I wouldn't know if she was dead or alive. My mom has tried to reach out to me, but I don't want to look at a drug addict. When she gets her life together, then we can work on our relationship. If I'm as important to her as she says I am, she'll straighten out her life. It's been twelve years since I last saw her, so I really ain't pressed about it anymore. She doesn't want to change. In my mind, she doesn't exist.

For the next few years, after we moved in with Auntie Whitley, things were good. Living with

Auntie Whitley brought a sense of stability back into our lives. She treated Russell and me as if we were her kids. Under her tutelage, we all excelled in school and sports. She wouldn't accept anything less. She kept us busy in sports to keep us off the streets.

I overlooked the fact that she ran through niggas like it was nothing—never mind the fact I could hear her getting her pussy beat out of the frame, night in and night out. I guess her pussy was good, because that's what kept the niggas around. Outside of that, once the sex got stale, the niggas bounced. Auntie couldn't keep a man to save her life.

Things were good until March 13, 2008. That date forever changed my life. I was fourteen. Russell was sixteen and in the eleventh grade; Tacari was a seventeen-year-old high school senior. It was a late Wednesday afternoon and we were in the middle of spring break, dreading going back to school the following week. The three of us had been out of the house all day, playing basketball. The local radio station was having some block party later that night and auntie said we could go. We got back home from playing basketball in enough time to shower and eat before going to the block party. As soon as we walked in the house, Auntie Whitley said, "I need y'all to go the dollar store and get some rice and green beans for my dinner. I forgot to pick them up."

She's always missing something when she cooks. It never fails. Somebody always has to go back out to get something.

"Ight, mama," Tacari said, as we rushed back

to his car. My cousin worked hard the last summer, saving all his money, to get this old, white, big-body, Chevy Caprice. Shit, we didn't care how old the car was...we wasn't walking or catching the bus anymore.

After we grabbed the stuff she needed from the dollar store, Tacari said, "It's gonna be a minute before she finishes dinner. I gotta grab something to snack on."

"Why didn't you get something out of the dollar store?" Russell looked at Tacari.

"Shit, I want some chips or something," I added, from the backseat.

"Let me stop at the corner store, right quick," Tacari said, as he pulled into the parking lot. "Y'all staying in here or getting out?"

"I'm coming," I replied.

"Leave your windows down," Russell said, as the new Lil Wayne CD played. "It's hot and the AC doesn't work. I'm gonna stay in the car. Y'all hurry up."

I got out of the car and rushed inside the store. Tacari's ass was always indecisive on what he wanted. I grabbed a king size bar of the white chocolate Kit Kat and a fruit punch. As I approached the checkout line, I looked back, and Tacari was still trying to figure out what flavored chips he wanted. I nodded my head, as I reached in my pocket and gave the cashier the money. When I got my change, I grabbed my candy and juice. I looked at Tacari and said, "Hurry up, man. We don't wanna be outside all day waiting on you. It's just chips, nigga."

"Take yo' lil ass on somewhere," he nodded his head, as he snatched up a bag of salt-n-vinegar chips.

"Bout damn time, nigga," I laughed, walking to the exit door. When I opened the door, it seemed as if everything went in slow motion.

I jumped in shock, as the food and drink slid out of my hands and onto the ground. I screamed at the top of my lungs, as I witnessed bullet after bullet enter my brothers' body. I witnessed my brothers' murder.

Pop, pop, pop, pop, pop, pop, pop, pop, pop.

The sound of those gunshots still rings in my head.

He had the gun pointed directly at Russell's chest. I watched that nigga unload his gun into my brother. He killed Russell in broad daylight, got in the get away car and sped off.

Tacari and I ran to Russell. It served no purpose; he was already dead. I can still feel his blood on my hands. I cried, as I held Russell's lifeless body in my arms. When I think about it, it often reminds me of that scene from Boyz in da Hood, when the Ricky, played by Morris Chestnut, was murdered leaving the convenience store. I felt just like Cuba Gooding, Jr, crying, holding his dead best friend in his arms. Not only was Russell my brother, he was *my* best friend, too.

Even though I knew who murdered my brother, I couldn't prove it because I never saw his face. I only saw the backside of his body. That fuck nigga never went to jail for it. That haunted me for years—and at times, it still does. One of my reoccurring nightmares is that fuck nigga is gonna come back to kill me, too.

My brother died over stupid shit. Turns out,

that grown ass man killed my brother, because my brother was fucking his girlfriend. My brother was sixteen. That girl was sixteen. What the fuck is a twenty-five year old dude, fucking a sixteen-year-old girl in the first place? That girl and my brother went to high school together. That fuck nigga was...is...a notorious drug dealer in the neighborhood; so, I guess he had to show his crew he doesn't get fucked over. I guess he had to show his authority. I knew other people at the store saw his face; but, because he is who is, they were scared for their lives, too. No one ever came forward and said anything to the police.

I can't get those memories out of my mind. My stepdad blowing his brains out. My brother. I can't get that image...seeing my brother...gunned down. My grandmother never waking up. Me shaking her body, but it was as hard and cold as a bag of ice. Watching my mother snort that shit, watching her shoot that mess up her arms. It haunts me. It all haunts me. No child should have to endure what I've endured. Shit isn't fair. I've seen more blood as a child, than someone fifty years old.

This is why I blame, you, God. You've taken everything away from me. My stepdad-gone. My mom-gone. My grandmother-gone. My brother-gone. Then, on top of everything, I'm a fucking faggot!

I don't wanna be a damn faggot. I fuck niggas! Who in their right mind would willingly want to fuck a dude? That shit is unnatural. Yet, I can't help it. Men is who and what I like. Why don't I have an attraction to females? Why can't they make my dick hard? Why am I this way? Why do

Bad Religion

I like dudes? What the fuck is wrong with me? What did I do to you God, that you hate me like this? What did I do to you? Huh? I did everything I was supposed to do. I did everything right.

I was raised in the church. I was in the choir. I studied the bible. I was active in the community. Whatever the pastor wanted, I did. Even if I didn't want to do it, auntie made me do it. The bible tells me I was made in *your* image. So, why the fuck am I a faggot? You said being gay is an abomination. So, why did you make me like this? What do you want from me? Why am I like this? Why can't I change? You created me to send me to hell?

Fuck you!

You've taken everyone I love away from me, and then topped it off by making me a homosexual. And Silas wonders why I won't get close to him. Everyone I get close to leaves me. I'm tired of being hurt. I'm tired of the pain. I'm tired, man. I'm tired. Niggas only see me as a piece of meat. Nobody wants to get to know me, everybody just wanna fuck. Silas ass, too. He just wants the fucking dick, too. I want kids. That shit ain't gonna happen because my dick won't get up for a bitch. Where did I go wrong? What am I being punished for? Damn, I wish Russell were here. I miss my brother, man. I fucking miss my brother.

Yeah, I gotta nice car. Yeah, I play college basketball. Yeah, I can pull niggas and bitches. Yeah, I gotta nice body. But nobody knows the real me. Nobody knows my story. Nobody knows the pain I'm in. Nobody knows how all of this shit has controlled my mind, my thoughts, my actions—my life. I just want to be free. I just want to be free from all of this. I want my brother back. I just want Russell back. I want my mind back. I wanna be straight. I wanna be normal. I want this curse lifted off me.

Fuck this, man. Fuck all of this shit. I'm so over this. I wish someone would just take me out of my misery. *Please.*

12

Auntie Whitley's music woke me up. *Some shit never changes.* When we were coming up, she blasted gospel music every Sunday morning, waking up the damn neighborhood. This morning, Kurt Carr was the designated gospel artist. *Jesus Can Work it Out,* was the active song on the playlist.

I laid in bed for a few more minutes, and then exhaled before forcing myself out of bed. I still had on my clothes from yesterday. How the hell did I get under the covers? Damn, I must have been tired. I hate sleeping in my street clothes. That shit is uncomfortable. *Whatever.*

I placed my luggage on the bed and searched through it, until I found my black slacks. I grabbed my light blue, long-sleeved dress shirt. I searched through my bag, trying to find my tie. *Fuck, I must have left it in the apartment back in Atlanta.* I walked over to my closet. I knew I had some ties in here. I grabbed a yellow and dark blue striped tie. I compared it to my shirt. *It's gonna have to work today.*

With my outfit laid out on the bed, I grabbed my toiletry bag and headed into the bathroom. I brushed my teeth and washed my face. I looked in the linen closet and retrieved a fresh washcloth and towel. While in the shower, I thought about last night. I hate when I get all emotional. I try my best not to put my problems on other people. I don't want anyone to look at all of my unfortunate circumstances and start to pity me. I don't need pity. I just want answers. I want my brother back. I know all of that is a pipedream. God has yet to answer any of my questions and I'm sure it won't be any time soon before he starts talking. It is what it is.

I got out of the shower, wrapped the brown towel around my waist, and headed back to my room. After I put on a fresh pair of red boxer briefs, I turned on the iron and prepared my clothes. After I put on my outfit, I stared at myself in the full-length, door mirror. Everything was looking good and in place. I slapped some grease on my head and brushed my hair. After I put on my gold wrist bracelet, I grabbed my wallet, phone and keys, and headed out of the room.

Kurt Carr's *The Presence of the Lord is Here* was now playing. I could hear my auntie singing along with the track...*even though she knows she can't sing worth shit.*

I reached the kitchen and it was smelling good. She had been in here cooking this morning. I grabbed the box of Frosted Flakes and fixed myself a hearty bowl. I sat down at the small circular kitchen table, munched on my cereal and looked at my Facebook, Twitter and Instagram profiles.

A few minutes into it, I looked up and saw my cousin walking into the kitchen with nothing but his boxers on.

I smiled.

"Waddup, cuz," he grinned from cheek-to-cheek, as we dapped each other up.

"Shit, what's up with you, Tacari?"

"Cuz, you know how it is. Trynna keep these hoes off my dick."

I chuckled and said, "I feel you on that."

He grabbed an omelet pan and put it on the stove. As he opened the frig to grab the eggs, cheese and ham meat, he said, "I tried to holla at you last night when I got in, but you were knocked the fuck out. I mean, damn, nigga, you was tired or sumthin'? You was in there stretched out across the bed, snoring loud as fuck. I was like damn, cuz tired as fuck. I helped you get under the covers. I tried to get you to take off your clothes, but you was gettin' mad at me 'n shit. I was like ight then, fuck nigga. I'll leave yo' ass alone." He laughed. Tacari looked at me and said, "You was tired, cuz?"

"Bruh, you have no idea."

Tacari Johnson felt like the only nigga I had left on my side, besides Renzo. I wanted to tell my cousin I was gay, but I'm not sure how he'll take it. Even though I'm the youngest, everyone looks up to me as if I'm the golden child. My cousin, Lexi, went to FAMU, but she didn't finish. She married some nigga and got like three kids with him. I swear her husband, Dwight, is DL, too. Something about that nigga just doesn't sit right with me. I guess the feeling is mutual because he keeps his distance, too. It's a shame because my cousin and her family lives in Atlanta, but I barely see them. Whenever we do get up, it's over lunch or something.

Tacari was a lil pretty, mama's boy. They argue and fight like cats and dogs, but they love each other. I think they're dependent on each other. That's why he won't leave and that's why she won't let him go—even though she's been threatening to kick him out since I was sixteen.

Tacari was 5'11" with dreads that extended past his shoulders. He always kept that shit nice and clean. Hell, one of them bitches he fuckin' keeps his hair on point. He had a caramel skin complexion and a lil muscle mass. Most of that came from when he played football in high school. He doesn't work out everyday like me, but he keeps himself in good shape. Unlike me, Tacari already had three kids by three different women. That first kid fucked him over. He was set on going to college. He had a full ride to the historically black school, Savannah State University, but the girl he was fucking around with at the time, got pregnant. He felt he couldn't go to college because he had to take care of his kid. That was admirable, but he didn't have to give up his scholarship. I'm sure auntie would have tried to help out as much as she could. So, he never went to college. He got a dead end job and has been working there ever since. This nigga lost all his motivation. He's just here, wasting away. It's sad, but everyone must chose their own path in life. I guess the only thing he thinks he's good for is making babies. There's been way more than three pregnancies—the other four females just had abortions. Think about that. He could be a father of seven—from seven different women. Craziness. Auntie Whitley doesn't know about them. No disrespect to my cuz, because I love him—but if I were a woman, I wouldn't be fucking no nigga that still lives at home with his mama. I don't care how sexy he may be, that shit wouldn't fly with me. But, when I look at the hoodrats he's fucking, they don't care about that shit. They just need the babies so they can continue to leech off the government. *Basic ass hoes.*

As he made his omelet, he said, "So, mama dun drugged ya' ass to church with her, huh?"

"Yep," I swallowed my milk. "Why ain't you going?"

"I gotta *work.*" He grinned.

"That's a damn shame," I nodded my head. "You should come with me so I won't be bored. "

"Naw, cuzzo, you on ya' own. Ain't nobody got time for that shit, man."

"That's fucked up, Tacari. You 'posed to be looking out for me."

"I'll make it up to you, but I ain't going to church."

I got up and washed out my bowl. Auntie didn't play about having dishes in her sink. As I sat back down, I heard the music stop playing. A few moments later, she walked in.

Auntie Whitley looked at Tacari with disgust and said, "I dun told yo' ass about walking around my house in your God damn drawers. Put some fucking clothes on, boy!"

"Yeah, I hear you, mama," he placed the omelet on a plate.

I looked at Auntie in her dark green pantsuit.

She managed to put some fresh weave in her hair this morning. She had it pulled into a ponytail. She looked at Tacari and said, "I know one damn thing, you betta not have them nasty ass bitches in my house. I know you ain't going to work. I ain't stupid, Tacari. I just don't have time to argue with yo' ass today."

He sat down, across from me, looked at his mom and said, "You 'bout to go to church, but you 'round here doing all that cursing."

She flicked him off and said "God knows my heart. Instead of worrying about what I'm doing or saying, you need to be finding ya' ass somewhere to live. You a grown ass man still living with his Goddamn mama. Done went and worked my damn nerves this morning." She sat down and pulled out a Newport. She placed the cigarette in her mouth and said, "Speaking of that, you got my money for the lights this month?"

"Ma, I'll get it to you, damn!"

I don't get these two. Never have, probably never will. She enables this behavior. She allows this to go on, so why complain? She created that lazy ass bum. I love my cousin, but he needs to get out of his mama's house. That shit is not a good look. Auntie probably needs Tacari. I think black women unconsciously use their boys for emotional, selfish reasons. Let that boy go. He is not your dick supply. He is not your husband or your boyfriend. He is not a little kid, anymore. Black women enable this culture that continues to create sorry ass black men. I'm so happy I'm trying to at least better myself, and not fall into that same trap that has incarcerated the minds of our black men.

She lit the cigarette, looked and me and said, "Well, good morning, Bryce. Don't you look good."

Damn, I can't stand the smell of smoke. "Auntie, you need to stop smoking. That ain't good for you. You gonna end up with lung cancer or something."

"We all gotta die of something," she checked the time, brushing me off.

She took a few more puffs then put the cigarette out. She reached in her purse, grabbed a bottle and started to spray it over herself, to help get rid of the smoky smell.

"C'mon, Bryce, before we're late," she stood up.

"Ight, cuzzo," Tacari grinned. "Say a prayer for me."

I got a prayer for his ass, alright. Making me go to church by myself.

She looked at Tacari and stated, "I got my roast in the oven. Keep an eye on it. If my shit burn up, I'm gonna burn yo' ass."

He rolled his eyes.

"You hear me, you lil yella nigga?" she stated.

"Ight, mama," Tacari drenched his omelet in syrup. "I hear you, damn. Go to church before you're late."

Just as she was gonna say something back to him, I interjected, "C'mon, Auntie Whitley, let's go."

"Jesus, be a fence," she mumbled, walking towards the front door. "I'm gonna kill that boy myself."

I smiled as I walked outside. Damn, you gotta love family.

13

As I got out of my car, I dreaded walking into this church. This was my childhood church. I got baptized here. I also found my first boy crush here, too. Nothing came of it, though. I was too scared to say anything.

"What's wrong with you, boy?" my aunt glanced at me.

"Nothing," I lied.

As we walked inside the church, the praise and worship team was going through one of their routines to Richard Smallwood's *Total Praise*. The ushers handed us a program. I followed my aunt to her usual seat. She's been sitting on this same pew since I was eight. Just as I was sitting down, my phone started to vibrate. It was the dude from Atlanta. I sighed and ignored his call. Just like when I was a child, my aunt reached into her purse and slid me a peppermint.

Before long, the eleven o'clock service had began. I looked around and there was a decent congregation here, today.

Jaxon Grant

When I was a kid, I did everything possible to make church fun. Listening to the choir always excited me, but that was about it. Well, then again, I used to get a kick out of watching this old lady catch the Holy Ghost...or *get happy*...as my auntie used to call it. Tacari, Russell and I, used to wait every Sunday to watch her yell, scream and run up and down the aisles. The ushers would catch her and cool her down with the paper fans that had Martin Luther King, Jr. face on it. Then, there was one Sunday when she *got happy*, fell and busted her ass. I got a good ass whipping that day, from Auntie Whitley, because I burst out laughing—and I couldn't stop. That phony ass lady deserved it. Everybody in the church knew she was faking. You can't catch the Holy Ghost *every* Sunday. Seriously. How ironic was it that, after she fell, she stopped doing that shit, too. I guess God taught her ass a lesson. Outside of listening to the choir and watching the actress perform her Holy Ghost skit, church was boring. Whenever the preacher started to preach, Tacari, Russell and I, would use the program and play games. We used to play hangman, tic-tac-toe and write jokes about the old ladies in the church. Man, I miss those days.

I miss Russell so much. Words can't describe the relationship that we had. Even though he was only two years older than I was, he protected me as if I was *his* son. Russell always made sure I never went without. Even when mama started to get fucked up on that crack, he made sure I had dinner every night—even if it was only a peanut butter and jelly sandwich. He tried his best to help me with my homework. He took whippings

104

for me. When I used to have nightmares as a kid, he would get in the bed and sleep with me. He loved me so much. Even as we got older, he was still there. He taught me how to lift weights. He taught me about girls and sex. He taught me the importance of saving money. Russell was my everything. We had been through so much together as kids, that we had a special bond. No one would ever understand the love that we had for each other. That was my brother.

I sighed.

Snap back into it, Bryce. Get it together.

During service, I occasionally looked around the church to see who was in here. I spotted a lot of females. Most of them had children with them. Where were their men? What's up with all these faggots in here?

During one of my random scans of the church, my eyes locked in on a phat ass, stuffed in some brown slacks. He was standing up, holding a baby during the alter call. While the pastor was praying, he turned his head and we locked eyes. I lifted my head—saying *what's up*—he lifted his back, acknowledging me. I did a quick glance to make sure no one saw the exchange. We were supposed to be praying.

He was sexy as fuck and appeared to be masculine. His skin tone was rich and chocolate, like actor Lance Gross. He had strong cheekbones, a fresh edge and a neatly trimmed chinstrap beard that was connected to his thin mustache and goatee. Based on the way his yellow dress shirt fit his body, I knew he worked out. His muscular thighs weren't helping my case. Strong, thick thighs, was my second weakness behind a strong, phat ass.

When the alter call was over, I watched him head back to his seat. He sat next to some female. He handed her the baby. She started to kiss the baby. I watched her whisper something in his ear. He smiled. My gut told me that was either his wife, or at the very least—his girlfriend.

While the choir sang their next song, he kept looking back over at me...on the sly. We locked eyes a few times. That nigga was making my dick hard in church. This is the wrong time for that shit—I have on slacks and my auntie is sitting right next to me. I love showing off my dick, but not sitting next to my auntie at church.

After the choir finished, some old woman with a big pink hat, came to the microphone to make the church announcements and to acknowledge any visitors. Once she was done, the pastor stood up and opened the floor for any testimonies.

I looked at my phone. I was past ready to go. Black churches know how to stay in church all damn day.

I glanced up when I heard a familiar voice say, "Giving honor to God, who's first in my life." *Oh great, Ms. Hattie was talking. This was easily gonna be a thirty minute speech.* My auntie mumbled something under her breath. I chuckled.

She continued, "To Pastor Williams, all the associate pastors, deacons and deaconesses. To the choir and the ushers and all of the congregation. Ain't...God...good?"

I heard a bunch of "Amen's," escape throughout the building.

"Pastor Williams, I just gotta tell you my story."

"Well gon' head, Mother Hattie," the pastor egged her on.

"Yesterday, when I got home, I pulled up in my driveway and said, 'Oh, my Jesus.' Pastor and church, Brother Bryce was getting out of his car."

OMG, she is about to embarrass me. My auntie playfully hit me on the side of my thigh.

"I was so happy to see him. He's doing very good over there at the college."

The college.

"When I see our young black boys like Brother Bryce, doing great things in they lives, we should all be proud. He could be in prison, selling drugs, or sleeping in his grave. The Lord is watching over Brother Bryce, and I think we should, too. Pastor, y'all know I can talk all day and all night and tomorrow too, but I'm gonna hurry on up now. I just wanted to say, I think we should hold a special offering for Brother Bryce, so he can have some extra money to take back over there to the college. We gotta support our family. Brother Bryce is family. Brother Bryce stand on up, so you can be acknowledged."

I exhaled and stood up. I glanced at the dude in the brown slacks. He looked back at me, and ran his tongue over his lips.

Ms. Hattie said, "He's playing basketball at the college. He's gettin' good grades at the college. He's gonna be grad'ating soon." She stared clapping and grinning from cheek-to-cheek.

"Let's give Brother Bryce a round of applause," Pastor Williams interjected. The church started to join in on the clapping. "I agree with Mother Hattie, we should reward Brother Bryce for his hard work. Matta fact, we need to make plans to have a college night here at the church. All monies raised will be split amongst our college students from the church." The pastor looked at one of the deaconesses and said, "Sister White, can you get working on that for me?"

"Yes, Pastor, I'll get right on it."

"Y'all make sure y'all drop a couple of extra dollars in the special collection plate for Brother Bryce," the pastor said. "Brother Bryce, would you like to say anything?"

I cleared my throat. "I'm not a man of many words, but I just want to thank y'all for all the love and support. I really appreciate it." I sat down.

As the pastor continued to talk, I glanced back over to dude in the brown slacks. When the choir started to sing their next song, he looked back at me and we locked eyes, yet again. I was tired of playing this game. He knew what the deal was. I waited patiently for him to look back, again. I saw him talk to the young woman who was sitting next to him. I eyed him nod his head to the sounds of the choir. Then, he did it again.

Without wasting any time, I stood up and said to my aunt, "I've gotta use the bathroom. I'll be back."

I eased past her and into the center aisle. I walked towards the back exit door. I smiled at the usher and went outside.

Hopefully, he got the hint to follow me. I waited for a few moments. Then, I heard the door open. I turned around and it was him. No words were spoken. I motioned for him to follow me.

I headed for the church annex. Once inside, I headed to the back. That's where all the offices were held. Nobody is back here during service on Sundays. I could hear the choir still singing their hearts out. I never looked back. I could hear his footsteps following behind me.

I opened the door to the one-person bathroom. It was directly across from the pastor's office. He followed me inside. I closed and locked the door.

I never said anything. I leaned against the wall, unzipped my pants and pulled out my dick. He looked me in the eyes, then stared at my dick. It was getting harder by the second.

The choir stopped singing. We both waited. I could see the nervousness on his face. Pastor Williams blessed the offering. He even mentioned my name. Soon after, the choir started singing Kirk Franklin's old hit, Melodies from Heaven.

"So, what's up?" I whispered over the music.

He swallowed on his spit. I could see the nervousness on his face. Still, he fell to his knees and started to slurp me up. I knew I couldn't verbalize the pleasure, so I kept it inside by taking deep breaths and exhaling. I placed my hands over his head. I don't know why I did that...it just felt right. This definitely wasn't his first time sucking a dick. I lifted my dress shirt, right above my navel. I looked down at him. He was enjoying this big black dick, sliding in and out of his mouth. I thought back to his phat ass. I pushed him off my dick.

He looked up at me and said, "What's wrong?"

"After the final selection from the choir, the next voice you will hear will be none other than, Pastor Kendrick Williams," I heard the associate pastor state. Soon after, the choir started to sing Tamela Mann's inspirational hit, Take me to the King.

"Do you get fucked?" I pried.

"Yeah," he nodded his head.

"Turn around."

When he turned around, I grabbed his ass. My dick was throbbing. I unzipped his pants and let them fall to the floor.

I nibbled on his ear, while I eased his gray boxer briefs down. I turned him around, so he was facing the wall. I leaned him over and kneeled down to his ass. I did a quick smell test by running my index and middle fingers through his ass crack. I needed to make sure this nigga was clean. I don't fuck shitty assholes. He passed my smell test, so I spread his cheeks a part. I stuck my tongue inside. His body shivered at my touch. I licked around, getting it good and wet. Eating this nigga out was making me hornier than ever. The fact that we were in church, made it even more enticing. Fucking in church—during church services, nonetheless—had to be a cardinal sin. But fucking a nigga...that shit guaranteed my seat, on a first class flight, to the pits of hell.

"Can I fuck right quick? That ass phat as fuck nigga."

He stood up and said, "I need to be getting back inside. I don't want nobody to come looking for us."

"It'll be quick, I promise."

He exhaled, as if he was thinking everything over—weighing the pros and cons of the situation. "You gotta condom?"

"Naw, but I'm clean," I pleaded.

"Naw, bruh," he shook his head. "I can't do it without a condom. I gotta wife and a kid, bruh."

I sighed. "Can you just finish me off, then? I'm

rock hard."

As he resumed sucking me off, I focused on getting this nut. I knew we had been back here to long when I heard Pastor Williams speaking. Thinking about his wife and child, I pulled out. I wasn't in the mood to get off anymore. I didn't want no fucking mop job, I wanted some ass.

"What's wrong?" he looked up to me.

"Nuthin', bruh, I'm good," I snatched a paper towel to wipe off my dick.

"I do something wrong?" he stood up, fixing his clothes.

"Naw," I put my dick back in my pants. "We have been back here a long time. If you wanna get up later, I'm home for the week, so just holla at me. Shoot me a text so I can save you in my phone."

"That's what's up" he said, as I gave him my ten digits. "Don't be hitting me up at late hours. I gotta family and I don't need no issues."

"Trust me, I'm not gonna hit you up at all. I understand the game. I know how nosy women are. If you wanna get up, you'll hit me up."

A few moments later, I got his text. I input his name as *Brown Slacks* and saved him as a new contact.

"You should go back in before me," I said. "I'll wait around here then go back inside."

"Ight," he exhaled. He looked at himself in the mirror to fix his clothes. He took another deep breath, opened the bathroom door and walked out.

After about five, long, excruciating minutes, I headed back inside. I don't know why I was so nervous. As I walked down the aisle, I felt like all eyes were on me. My auntie looked over to me as I sat down. She cleared her throat, but didn't say anything. The pastor was in the middle of his sermon.

"I was twelve when my mother died giving birth to my baby sister," Pastor Williams said. "My mother was thirty-eight years old. For years, I didn't understand. I questioned God. I hated God."

Those words struck. My attention was peaked.

He continued, "Yes, I said it. I hated God. My father tried to make me understand, but none of it made sense. I can't repeat the words I said to God. I cursed him. Why would God take my mother from me, from us? I was still a boy. Why would God allow a baby to grow up, never knowing her mother? How could I not hate God, for what he's taken from me? I didn't understand and I hated him for it."

My body was tense. Was God talking to me? Was he finally speaking to me, through Pastor Williams? Is he about to answer my questions?

"Proverbs three, verses five and six says, 'Trust in the Lord with all your heart and lean not on your own understanding; in all your ways submit to him and he will make your paths straight.'"

The pastor took a sip of water.

He continued, "God is saying trust him. Despite our own ignorance, trust him. He will never lead you down the wrong path. I've learned everything in life happens for a reason. Our job is to figure out that reason and how that lesson can apply to our respective lives."

He looked directly at me. "I know this message is short. If I can be honest, this wasn't what I had planned to talk about today. However, during morning services, God spoke to me. He told me to speak about my mother and speak from my heart. He told me that someone here, today, needed to hear this message. God loves you. Despite our faults, God loves you. He hears you. He understands you. He is there for you. Don't give up. Don't give in. Remain strong. Pray. Get on your knees and pray. Resubmit yourself to Christ. Open your arms and allow him back into your life. He forgives. He loves. He is waiting for you. Just remember, the Lord will never put more on you than you can bear. The doors of the church are open."

Before the pastor dismissed the congregation, he asked that Auntie Whitley and I meet with him after church. I just wanted to get out of here.

When service was over, I followed my auntie over to him. I tried my best to keep my face in my phone, because I really didn't feel like talking to anyone. As usual, there was a line waiting to speak to the pastor.

A few minutes later, we approached him. Pastor Kendrick Williams was a nice looking man. He was probably in his mid-forties. He looked to be in pretty good shape. He had a baldhead with a mustache and connecting goatee. He took over the church when his father dropped dead of a massive heart attack. I think I was the tenth grade when that happened. His wife stood next to him. She was beautiful. Even though women do nothing for me sexually, I love looking at a strong, beautiful, black woman. Something about powerful black women is sexy to me. His wife, Dr. Jillian Williams, was a dean at Savannah State

University.

"It's so good to see you, Bryce," she reached over and hugged me. "Is everything going ok at Clark?"

"Yes, ma'am," I forced a smile. "Everything is good." I glanced at the pastor. Even though he was talking to my aunt, I felt like he was burning a hole in my shirt, staring at me.

"That's good," she put her attention on my aunt.

The pastor extended his hands and said, "It was a pleasant surprise to see you here today, Brother Bryce."

"Yes, sir, I got back in town last night."

"I'm glad you deemed it worthy to give the Lord some of your time." He pulled me to the side and said, "You know, if there is anything you wish to talk about, I'm here."

"Everything is good, Pastor Williams," I forced a smile.

He looked me up and down, then said, "Oh, here is the collection from earlier. I haven't counted it, but I know it's a pretty good amount in there. I dropped a hundred in there myself."

"Wow, thanks, Pastor Williams."

He stared at me again. It was as if he wanted to say something, but was afraid. *What the fuck is up with that?* The fact that he knew God was telling him to speak to me is creepy as fuck. I hope this man isn't some prophet. I hope he can't see through me. I hope he can't see the sexual activities that went down in his church today. I hope he isn't judging me, calling me all kinds of homosexual slurs in his mind. That has to be why he's looking at me like this.

When my auntie and Dr. Williams finished talking, I exhaled. After we said our goodbyes and prepared to walk away, the pastor said, "Brother Bryce, hopefully we'll see you back in here next Sunday before you go back go Atlanta."

"Ight, I'll be here," I smiled, as I turned around and headed out of the church.

I rolled my eyes and thought to myself, "*Wait on it, nigga.*"

14

As soon as I got back home, I went in the room and counted the money the church collected for me.

"$372...not bad," I smiled. I can definitely make good use of that money.

I took off my clothes and put on some black balling shorts, a black wife beater and my black ankle socks.

I laid down on the bed. That nigga at church got me horny as fuck. I need to bust this nut off in a tight hole. I thought about Silas. I was starting to miss him a little bit. *Naw—I'm just horny as hell.*

I grabbed my tablet out of my book bag and turned it on. I knew what I was going to do, but I knew I didn't need to do it. Once the tablet was up and running, I immediately went to the m4m section of Craigslist and posted an ad. I titled it, *Looking to fuck ASAP.* In the body of the ad, I wrote, "A nigga trying to get up in some ass ASAP. I'm black, masculine, athletic and sexy...you must be too. For the idiots that can't read that means no fats, no fems or anything else in between. Oh yeah, no oldies either. I ain't trying to fuck my daddy. You must be black. That's just how I roll. If you can't take some serious black pipe, don't waste my damn time. If you don't like my requirements, fuck you. If you're not black, I may make an exception if ya ass is phat enough. Masculine niggas with phat asses only. You see a pic of my dick...make sure you send a pic of your ass in the first message. Make sure it's titled 'Phat Azz'. If that's not there, in the subject line, I'm not even opening the message... just gonna delete it. Trust, I'm on point. If you can meet those requirements, fuck with me. If not, fuck off. You must host."

I attached two of my dick pics then submitted the ad.

Just as I got the email alert on my phone, saying the ad was posted, I turned on the TV. Basketball was on. Chicago and Miami were playing. During the game, I kept checking my phone to make sure I didn't miss any emails. There was nothing. I also played around on Instagram and Twitter.

About an hour into watching the game, there was a knock on my door. Before I could say anything, Tacari peeped his head inside the room. I looked at him.

"Mama said the food is done. Come on out here and eat."

"Ight," I jumped up, turning off my TV.

When I got in the kitchen, Auntie Whitley was cutting up the pork roast.

"That smells good, Auntie," I kissed her on the

cheek.

"It's gonna taste even better," she smiled.

She fixed our plates and handed them to us. On the menu were pork roast, rice and gravy, collard greens, potatoes, garden salad and cornbread. To top it off, she made my favorite dessert—sweet potato pie.

"Why don't you cook like this for me?" Tacari quizzed his mom, as we ate.

"Because you're a lazy ass nigga that owes me money."

I laughed and said, "Boy, y'all two stay at it."

"She loves me though," Tacari said.

"I love you, but I don't gotta like ya' ass," Auntie Whitley nodded her head.

Tacari rolled his eyes.

She continued, "Pastor Williams gave a heartfelt sermon today."

"Yea, it was cool," I replied.

"Speaking of church," she dived in. "What took you so long to come from the bathroom?"

I looked at her and lied, "I had to do number two and then I got a phone call. I didn't realize I was gone that long."

"Umm, hmm," she looked at me. "That other man was gone for a long time, too. You left, and then he left. Both of y'all were gone for a very long time. Then he came back in, and you came back in five minutes later. I could have sworn I saw him looking back at you a couple of times during church. Well, he was looking at somebody in our area. Coincidence, ain't it?"

I shrugged my shoulders before taking a sip of my drink. *Was she trying to tell me she knew something?*

She ate some of her greens then said, "I know he's married with a baby, but I think that boy is gay."

"Who?" Tacari's interest was peaked.

"Melvin," Auntie Whitley said.

"Melvin Turner? He's married to Keisha, and they got a new baby, right?" Tacari asked.

"Umm, hmm, that's him," Auntie nodded her head, in her gossiping tone.

"Oh, yeah, that nigga out of there. He's one of them DL niggas," Tacari took a sip of his tea. "People used to talk abut him when we were in high school. He looks like a nigga, but he a faggot. I don't know why Keisha married him. I know she had to hear the rumors when we were in school. After we graduated, one rumor stated he got caught sucking off one of the football players that graduated with us."

"Figures," my auntie looked at me.

"Why you looking at me like that?" I asked her.

"No reason," she smiled. She ate some of her roast, then said, "If you gonna be gay, be gay. I know I don't care. Just don't be messing up everybody lives in the process, because you're scared of what your family and friends might say. Black men are selfish."

"That shit is just nasty as hell," Tacari said. "All these beautiful, black women out here and niggas wanna fuck other niggas. That shit crazy, ain't it, cuz."

"Yeah—crazy, bruh," I nodded my head.

My auntie kept stealing glances at me. Shit was making me uncomfortable. Thankfully, Tacari changed the subject.

For some strange reason, that speeding ticket I

got yesterday popped in my mind. I thought about telling her about it. *Naw, I'll tell her once I'm back in Atlanta. I'll be safe that way. Now that I think about it, I can use that money the church gave me today, to pay that ticket. I'll still have a little over a hundred dollars to blow.*

When dinner was over, she had Tacari and I clean up the kitchen. I volunteered to do it by myself. I didn't want him bringing up that conversation with *Brown Slacks*...well Melvin...from church.

After I finished up, I headed back to my room to relax. I continued watching basketball. The Chicago/Miami game ended up going to overtime. Chicago pulled it out. Oklahoma City and the Lakers came on next. With Kobe being injured, the Lakers suck. This game was going to be a snooze fest.

I guess I had dozed off, because I woke up to my phone vibrating. I looked at the TV and the nightly news was on. I looked at my phone and that nigga from Atlanta was calling. I ignored the call. I saw that I had some emails. *Hopefully, something good is in here so I can bust this nut.*

I went through the emails and got pissed off. Why can't niggas follow directions? I clearly said to send an ass pic in the first email. *Delete.*

I looked at another email. That ass is not phat. *Delete.*

This nigga didn't even title it correctly. I opened the mail just to see the picture. *Delete.*

My phone started to vibrate again. It was Silas. I ignored his call, too. I just wasn't in the mood for him.

I flipped through the TV until I reached a rerun

of the Real Housewives of Atlanta. Secretly, this shit was my addiction. These hoes are off the wall. Renzo and I watch this shit, faithfully, every Sunday. We couldn't get into the other Housewives franchises. But Atlanta, that ratchet ass mess was right up our alley—probably because they were black and we could instantly connect and relate to them. I don't fuck with the fags like that, but that damn Miss Lawrence...that punk look like he got some good ass. Then there's Kandi's fiancé, Todd. That nigga gay. I don't care what nobody says. That's probably why Mama Joyce can't stand his ass. I'll fuck him. Shit.

My phone went off. It was an email from Craigslist. I opened the ad, and looked that man's ass. *Hell fuck yeah!* Finally! I smiled. I replied back, "That's what's up. You gotta body pic?" I attached mine in the email.

A few moments later, he sent back a shot from the neck down. *Yeah, this can work.* I sent an email saying, "Cool. You got a free spot? How old are you?"

Within moments, he replied, "No, but I can get a hotel if you trying to get up tonight. I'm 46 years old."

When I read forty-six, my stomach churned and my dick went soft. I wasn't fucking no nigga twice my age, plus some. I replied, "I'm str8 bruh."

He sent, "What's wrong?"

I emailed, "You're old as fuck! Did you not read my ad? I clearly said no oldies. Don't worry about writing back...I'm just gonna delete it."

Damn, I can't stand these stupid ass niggas.

How hard is it to follow directions? *I'm just gonna jack off, watch Housewives and take my ass to sleep.*

Then it hit me. *Fuck, I can't jackoff here.* Auntie didn't believe in locking room doors. She could burst in at any moment.

Fuck, I need to get my ass back to Atlanta...ASAP!

15

Coming back to my old high school always made me feel good. Niggas knew me. I was a legend at this school. We won two state basketball championships because of me. I'll never forget the last game of my high school career. It was a scene right out of a movie. It was only a few seconds left in the game. The scores were tied and we had the final possession. Coach told us that if we missed the shot, it was ok because we'll go to over time. The play was designed for me. I felt confident. I knew I was going to hit that shot. When the ball was thrown to me, I held it at the top of the key, while my teammates cleared out the paint. It was just me and the defender. I glanced at the game clock. It was ten seconds left in the game. I eyed my defender. At seven seconds, I started to dribble the ball as I moved in towards the free throw line. Like Michael Jordan did in game six of the 1998 NBA Finals against the Utah Jazz, I did a crossover on my defender. He went for the steal. I pushed him off and as he fell down, I raised up for the jump shot. It felt like slow motion watching the ball spin in the air. Then, it fell straight through the hoop—nothing but net. That's how my senior year ended. A nigga left out on top.

The memories. Good memories.

I wish Russell were here to witness that important moment in my life. He taught me everything I knew about basketball. If he weren't killed, he'd probably be in the NBA by now. He was definitely a better basketball player than me.

After I checked in at the front office, I grabbed my visitor's pass and made my way to Coach Wyatt's office. I knocked on his door and stepped inside.

When he saw me, he said, "Well, it's about time you got here. I was starting to think you weren't coming."

"Naw, coach," I gave him a brotherly hug. "My auntie had me running some errands."

He laughed and said, "That Whitley knows she is something else. How is she doing?" he sat down. I sat down across from him, at his desk.

"She's good. Just my crazy behind auntie."

"She should be proud. She did a very good job with you."

Coach Wyatt was the father I never had. He was big. He was mean. He was tough. He was an in-your-face kind of guy. He pushed me to levels I'd never been.

He was about 6'7" and had the body of Lebron James. Coach played in the NBA for a few years, before a knee injury ended his career. He went back to college and finished his degree in education. He's been at my high school for at least fifteen years. He's a leader in the African

American community, here in Savannah. Everyone knows and loves Coach Wyatt.

I met him when I was twelve. Russell was a freshman on the varsity basketball team. *That's just how good he was.* I used to come to their practices after school. Since I was always around, Coach Wyatt let me be the assistant equipment manager for the team. I had to assist the head equipment manager in whatever tasks needed to be completed. I loved it. I rushed to Russell's high school as soon as my middle school was released. Luckily, the walk wasn't that far. I went to all of their games. I was part of the team. The players loved me. Sometimes, I even got to practice with them. Auntie Whitley was thankful for Coach Wyatt. He helped keep us off the streets and out of trouble.

"So, you said you needed to talk to me. What's going on, Bryce?"

"I'm not feeling it, anymore."

"Feeling what?" he asked, concerned.

"Basketball. I'm losing interest in playing ball. It's not fun, anymore. I just want to be a normal student."

"I understand," he nodded his head. "It can take a toll on you."

"Coach, I'm so close to telling my coach at Clark that I'm quitting the team. I just wanna be free."

"That wouldn't be a wise move," Coach Wyatt said. "I understand it may not be fun anymore, but this is about more than having fun. Bryce, you are receiving a college education, at the expense of Clark Atlanta University. Playing basketball is your job. You are a grown man, so only you can make your adult decisions. My advice to you, is be a man and tough it out. Use basketball as an avenue to a free college education. You're going to walk away from Clark with a degree and no student loan debt. Majority of America—especially young educated Black Americans—can't make that claim. Trust me when I say, having student loan debt is not what you want. Keep pressing on, taking it day-by-day, until you get that piece of paper in your hands. You're so close to the finish line. "

I stayed and chatted with coach for another hour or so. I left when he had to go do lunch room duty. Being around the high school atmosphere kind of made me miss it—for a split second.

I really didn't have anything planned for the rest of the day. I knew I wanted to stop by the mall and use some of the money the church gave me yesterday, to get some new shoes. I was a little hungry, so I figured I could kill two birds with one stone, while I was at the mall.

Before going to the mall, I drove around town to clear my mind. I knew I was wasting gas, but I needed this alone time away from everyone.

Yesterday's conversation with my aunt was bothering me. Was she letting me know, she knows or suspects I'm gay? Was that her way of telling me she doesn't care? The last thing I need is my family thinking I'm a fucking faggot. Maybe I need to produce a female love interest, so they can put that thought out of their head.

As I reached the mall, my phone lit up. It was Silas.

Reluctantly, I answered, "What's up?"

"Where you at? What'cha doing?"

I pulled the phone from my ear and stared at it. Did he not hear anything I said on Saturday? We're not together anymore, so he needs not be questioning my whereabouts.

"Hello, you there?" he asked.

"What do you want, Silas?"

"I want to talk about us."

"There is no more us," I stressed. "I need you to get that through your thick ass head."

"Bryce," he sighed.

"Silas, it's over."

"We've been through this, thousands of times before," he said. "It's not over. You always come back. So, I'm just trying to work it out now."

"Silas, you're sounding real needy right now. That shit is not a good look. Accept it. I'm done with you, man. I'm serious this time."

"You know what, fuck you, Bryce."

"Silas, I don't have time to listen to you curse me."

"Karma is gonna fuck yo' ass up. I've been nothing but honest and faithful to you, Bryce. I tried my best to make this relationship work and I don't know why. Time after time, you've shown me your true colors. I don't know why I continued to put up with your bullshit. I don't know why I'm trying to save this fucked up relationship, in the first place. You're so fucking bitter, Bryce. You're nasty. People think you're all nice and sweet, but nobody knows the real Bryce—that is until you're in a relationship with him. God is gonna punish you for the way you've treated me, for the things you've done to me. All the lying and cheating. All the arguments. Karma is gonna get your ass."

"Silas, I'm not about to listen to this. I'm done.

Do not contact me ever again. I mean that shit...don't fucking call me again. Matta fact, lose my damn number!" I hung up the phone.

Frustrated, I thought about sex. I needed to fuck. I needed to release this anger. Before I went inside the mall, I posted another ad on Craigslist. *Hopefully, the results are different this time.*

16

Once inside the mall, I headed directly to the shoe store. I knew the shoes I wanted, so there wasn't any need in wasting any extra time. After I got my shoes, I saw a shirt I liked. It was only twenty-four dollars, so I scooped that up, too. Buying clothes and shoes always made me feel better. It was my guilty pleasure. I headed over to the food court and ended up getting some Shrimp Lo Mein, from the Chinese booth.

While I ate my food, my emails started going off. I sighed. It was the same shit as last night. Why can't I find a good-looking young black man, with a phat ass, to fuck? I wish *Brown Slacks* would hit me up. I really wanna get in that ass.

I wish I knew where this attraction to dudes came from. From a child, I knew I was different. I didn't know what gay was, but I always knew I was different. I truly believe I was born this way. If I had a choice, I would be with a woman. That's natural. It's supposed to be that way. We're here to procreate. Two men can't make a baby, but women don't do shit for me. My dick just won't get hard for them. I've tried. I've had relationships with females during high school. I've fucked girls, but it does nothing for me. Thankfully, my dick is big enough so they can still get some pleasure out of it. I've never been fully erect, fucking a girl. For some strange reason, if I do get hard, it only last for a few seconds. That's how I know I'm gay. Pussy doesn't scare me...it just does nothing for me. Seeing a nigga sag his pants, showing the top of his ass—that shit makes my dick hard. It's a natural reaction to do a double take on a sexy ass nigga. Nia Long could be standing on a corner, butt ass naked, and I would keep walking. I just don't understand why God would make me this way.

Whatever, Bryce. There you go again...getting all into your feelings 'n shit. Man up, nigga. Man up.

I finished off my meal. As I took a sip of my drink, I received another email. He really wasn't my type, but I'm just horny as fuck right now. I stared at his picture and his stats. I wasn't fucking him, but I'll just let him suck me off.

I sent, "Yooo, I don't have time to fuck anymore...but if you wanna suck me off real quick I'm down."

He emailed back, "That's cool. I'm at the house by myself for a couple of hours. Slide thru."

Instantly, I got up from the table. I threw my trash out and headed back to my Charger. I placed my new shoes and shirt into the trunk. I input his address into my GPS and left the mall.

During the ride, I refused to think about what I was about to do. I knew if I thought about it, I would get disgusted at myself—for being desperate.

Once I parked my car, I grabbed my fitted hat and placed it on my head. I headed upstairs to his apartment. I knocked on the door and turned around so that my back was to the door. I didn't want him looking at my face, through the peephole for ten seconds, before opening the door.

When he opened the door, I exhaled then turned around. I lifted my head and walked inside. I stood in the foyer until he gave me directions.

I knew I was losing my fucking mind. This dude definitely *was not* my type. He wasn't fat, but he had a little weight to him. Fat niggas, thick niggas...whatever they call themselves...think their phat asses are hot. No nigga, your ass is *phat* because you're fat! You got an ass in the back and one in the front, too. Not sexy at all. Niggas asses be all soft like a bitch ass. Fucking cellulite every damn where. Disgusting. I wanna fuck a man's ass. I wanna see a muscle ass. I wanna see an ass without a gut attached. I'm all about saving money and getting discounts, but that's one, two-for-the-price-of-one, I don't want.

"You can sit down on the couch," he said.

I should leave. I'm not gonna enjoy this. Nigga, you're already here now. Just bust the nut and get out.

"You straight?" he asked.

"Yea, I'm good," I pulled off my shoes. I unbuttoned and unzipped my jeans. I took them off and placed them on the love seat. I took off my green boxer briefs and placed them on top of my jeans. I thought about removing my shirt, but I was gonna need that in a little bit to protect my face.

My dick was soft as fuck. Normally, when I'm about to get some head, I'm instantly on brick. That is a tell-tale sign that he isn't my type.

I grabbed my dick and sat down on the black couch. He kneeled down and reached for my dick. I looked down at him. He wasn't ugly or anything. Truthfully, there's nothing wrong with big dudes...but they're just not for me. Everybody has a type. I'm no different.

As he started working on getting me hard, I exhaled. *I can't believe I just lowered my standards. I can't believe I just settled, so I can get this nut off.* The things niggas do when they are horny. There must be some chemical in your brain that makes you lose all sense of judgment when you are horny. When your dick is talking, you'll do shit you normally wouldn't do. You'll fuck people, you normally wouldn't fuck. That's the power of sex.

Ight, Bryce, just lay back and relax. Ignore the nigga who's doing the sucking and just enjoy the pleasure.

I closed my eyes and concentrated. I placed my left hand on my abs, raising my shirt. As the pleasure started to consume my mind, I looked down and he was looking up at me. *That was awkward.*

There are unwritten rules in dick sucking. The first rule in sucking dick is *no fucking teeth.* The second rule in sucking dick is, *never look at the person receiving the pleasure.* That creates an uncomfortable moment of exchange for the receiver. The person receiving is free to look at the dick sucker. The visual of seeing your dick slide in and out of that mouth, comes with the territory of being on the receiving end of this sexual act. The dick sucker eyes should remain closed at all times. If their eyes must open, it must be focused on the dick, and just the dick. It's kinda like kissing. Who kisses with their eyes open?

I reached up and grabbed my fitted cap. I pulled it down, with the rim covering my forehead to my nose. I grabbed the bottom of my shirt and lifted it up to cover the rest of my face. I slouched down in the seat. I closed my eyes and focused. Yes, this thick dude was sucking me off, but the image in my head was Silas. I envisioned my fuck sessions with Silas. I could hear his moans. I could see his phat, muscular ass. I could see myself pulling on his dreads, as I drilled into that pretty hole.

Damn, my dick was hard as fuck. Thick dude was doing that shit. I refocused back to Silas. I can't start to count how many times we've had sex in two years. I know I told him in the car his sex wasn't shit to me, but I just said that shit in frustration. I said it to piss him off—to get a reaction out of him.

The truth is that Silas is the best sexual partner I've ever had. That nigga knew my body. He knew the places to touch. He knew how to please me. Damn, I love that boy. I love him so much, it hurts.

I could feel my dick starting to soften, so I changed the images over to Brown Slacks. I know that ass is nice and tight. I could see my dick sliding in and out that shit. I want that nigga to ride me. Hell yeah. That shit was gonna make me bust. The pictures in my mind were getting intense.

"Oh, fuck," I said.

I could feel my legs shaking. That nut was on its way out. A few moments later, I yelled, "Oh, fuck, nigga! I'm cuming!" He swallowed all of my kids. He waited until my dick stopped throbbing before he came off it. I removed the shirt from my face. I placed my fitted cap back on my head. He stood up and grabbed a towel. He handed it to me. I wiped my dick.

Suddenly, I felt remorseful. I felt disgusted. Instantly, I regretted doing this. *Look at this nigga. Ugh. What the fuck were you thinking, Bryce?* Without saying anything, I placed the towel back on the couch. I put back on my green boxer briefs, followed by my jeans. I tied up my shoes. I grabbed my phone and waited for him to lead me to the front door. As soon as he opened the door, I dipped out—never saying a word.

17

When I turned over, I squeezed my eyes. I glanced at my phone. My indicator light was going off. I looked at the time. It was almost six in the morning. I input my passcode, 0313. That was the month and date that Russell left this world.

I had some missed calls and text messages. That nigga from Atlanta called me again, last night. Renzo called, too. I made a mental note to hit Renzo back up, later today. Damn, I must have been tired as hell to miss all of these calls and messages. I'm usually a light sleeper and I can hear my phone vibrating against the nightstand. I guess being back at home, in your bed, makes everything different.

I had some notifications from that social media shit. I looked at my text messages. Silas sent me a text telling me he wasn't taking me back this time. *Delete.* Renzo hit me up a couple of times, asking what I was doing. Tacari sent me a text asking if his mom was sleep. *That nigga ain't up to no good.* I had some other messages from some people in Atlanta.

I looked at my email. I had a few replies to my newest Craigslist ad. I posted another ad after dinner, last night. I needed to fuck! I don't want anymore head, I want to fuck! Besides, I wanted and I needed to erase the image of that thick nigga sucking me off.

I deleted the first three messages. *Niggas can't read and follow directions.* When I got to the fourth email, I soon realized it was the oldie from two nights ago. He emailed, "Listen. I know what your ad says, but something about your ad has me on brick. I don't mess around with dudes often, but I do get the urge to have some dick in my ass every once in a while. I promise you my ass is tight as fuck. I have a place where we can do it. Yes, I am forty-six, but I don't look it. I take care of my body. I take care of myself. Lastly, I don't mind paying for what I want...get at me."

This nigga is gonna give me some money for da dick? Shit, I might have to rethink my position. I looked at the time he sent the message. It was a little after eleven last night. I exhaled. That shit sounded enticing, but this sleep sounds even better.

To get the process started, I replied, "I just got your message. Sounds interesting. How much $$$ you talking? Get at me when you get this."

I set my alarm for nine, and then placed the phone down on the nightstand. That would give me another three hours to sleep in. I'll deal with these niggas later.

18

I never really got back into a deep sleep. I more or less just laid in bed and fell in and out of sleep. Sometimes being lazy is the thing to do. Shit, it is spring break. I ain't supposed to do shit, anyway.

I grabbed my phone and cut off the alarm before it started ringing, seven minutes later. I checked my email and the oldie hadn't replied back. I placed my hands inside of my boxer briefs. It was a bad habit of mine to play with my pubic hair. Occasionally, I would touch my dick to make sure it was still there. *Why do men stick their hands inside their pants and touch themselves? Who started that practice? I remember Al Bundy doing it a lot on the TV show, Married with Children.*

Damn, I really didn't want to get out of bed. Each day I wake up, I know that's one less day I have of spring break. I wasn't ready to go back to school. On top of that, it's only two days until the six-year anniversary of Russell's murder. I know I'm gonna go out to the cemetery and spend some time with him. I just want him to know that I will always be there for him, just like he was there for me. I'll never forget my brother.

There was a slight knock on my door. Thankfully, I was under the covers. Before I could remove my hand from my playing around in my pubic hair, Auntie Whitley opened the door and stepped in the room.

She smiled and said, "I was just checking to see if you were up."

"Yeah, I've been awake for a while."

"Is everything ok with you?"

"Yes, ma'am," I sighed. "Russell is on my mind. Besides that, I'm just dreading going back to school."

"School? You still got another five days before you gotta go back to Atlanta," she said.

"I know, but it's still in the back of my head. Each day I wake up, I'm reminded that's one less day I have here with my family."

She smiled then said, "Boy, stop. Anyway, I'm about to head on to work. I've got a long day today, so it's gonna be late before I get home. There is still a little left overs I put in a Tupperware bowl for you. You can have that for lunch. You're gonna have to get your own dinner tonight, because I know when I get home, I ain't cooking. I am gonna make some lasagna tomorrow. I know you love my lasagna."

"Now, that's what I'm talking about," I smiled.

"Well, let me go before I'm late. When Tacari gets up, tell him that grass better be cut or that's his ass—and that nigga better not cut any of the flowers I just planted, if so, I know something."

"I'll let him know," I nodded my head.

"Ight, baby, I love you and I'll see you later. Behave yourself."

"Yes, ma'am and I love you, too."

She smiled, walked out and closed the door. I knew I wasn't getting anymore sleep, so I got on up. I grabbed my basketball shorts off the floor and slid into them. I headed for the bathroom to take care of my morning duties. After I brushed my teeth, I grabbed my phone and headed in the kitchen to fix a bowl of cereal.

I flipped on the small TV in the kitchen to ESPN, for the latest Sports Center episode. While I ate my frosted flakes, the oldie replied back to my email.

"I got $300 here at the house with me. If I'm giving you $300, I want to be fucked good."

This nigga is about to drop three hundred dollars in my lap, for some dick? Oh, hell yeah. Money talks, bullshit walks. I'll fuck the old man for that.

I sent back, "That'll work. You're not the police are you? I ain't trying to go to jail."

He sent, "LOL. No, I'm not the police. Send me a picture."

I replied, "Not without seeing yours first. Niggas play games."

A few moments went by and he sent, "Well, I guess we'll just see each other in person. I'm free from now until noon. So if we're gonna do this, start making your way to me."

I swallowed my milk, washed out my bowl and headed back to my room. I sent, "Ight, let me get in the shower and I'll hit you up. Are you ready now? Is your ass clean? I don't fuck shitty kitties. Make sure you get a good cleaning because my dick is long and thick. It is guaranteed to unclog, clogged assholes."

He sent back, "You talk a good game, lol. I hope you can perform that way. But, yes, I'm clean and ready to go right now. Hit me up when you're finished."

When I got out of the shower, Tacari was coming out of his room in nothing but some plaid boxers. With the towel wrapped across my waist, I said, "Auntie said you better cut the yard today or that's your ass. Oh, yeah, if you touch one of her flowers, she's gonna fuck you up."

"Man, I don't got time for mama and that bullshit. Ain't nothing wrong with the yard. She just be finding shit for me to do because she be bored."

"I hear you," I went back inside my room.

Being that I was just going to fuck some ass, I put on my basketball shorts and black wife beater. I sent him an email asking for his address.

While I waited, it hit me. Where the hell have I been? This can be very profitable for me—selling my dick. I'm very attractive. I've got body and dick. I love to fuck and I know niggas would pay to have a piece of me. *Why hadn't I thought of this earlier?* It damn sure beats working at the restaurant for tips from those rich, racist white people.

I followed his directions. He told me to park at the McDonalds and walk, the rest of the way. He said that he has nosy neighbors. At first, I wasn't feeling it. But then, that money stared speaking to me. The walk ended up being all of two minutes.

I had condoms and lube in my pocket, but I

really prefer not to use the condom unless he requires it. Sex just feels better natural.

I checked my phone to make sure I had the correct address. I walked up the sidewalk until I got to his front door. I ranged the doorbell.

I know the man said he was forty-six, but I was interested in seeing what his face looked like. Like normal, I turned away from the door so he wouldn't look at me. I wasn't giving him, or anyone else, an advantage.

When the door opened, I turned to face him. My mouth damn near fell to the floor. His body was frozen in place. Shit, I didn't care. Nothing surprises me these days. I just wanted this money. *Let me come on in, bust that nut and get paid for doing it. I ain't gonna tell nobody you like to get fucked.*

"Well, can I come in, or are you just gonna stare at me with the blank face?"

"Sorry, please, come inside," he closed and locked the door.

I followed him into the living room. This was my first time inside his home. Shit was nice. I saw all his family pictures. There were his plaques and awards his wife had won.

"You can't say anything," he begged. "Please don't say anything."

"Listen, Pastor Williams," I looked him in the eyes. "I just wanna bust this nut, get this money and be out. I'm not in the business of outing people. You do what you do, I do what I do. Besides, I'm already here now. I've seen you. You've seen me. Let's just do what we came here to do."

This explains why he was looking at me like

that after church on Sunday. And to think I thought he was reading me and calling me homosexual slurs.

"You promise you're not going to tell anyone. If the church found out I have sex with men—"

"Pastor," I cut him off. "You have my word, I'm not telling anyone. Your secret is safe with me. Besides, if I tell someone, I'd be telling on myself, too. Trust and believe that shit is not happening. Now, let me see that ass."

19

Finally.

I finally got some ass.

Pastor Kendrick Williams gave me a run for my money. That nigga was a beast. He was riding my dick as if he was at the rodeo. He took that pounding like a man. I burst a couple of nuts with him. Shit was that good.

Now, we're both laying in his bed, exhausted. The fucked up part about this is that his wife sleeps in this bed. He didn't even make me put on a condom.

I just fucked my pastor, in the bed he shares with his wife. Craziness. I know I'm going to hell, for real.

"What's on your mind?" he looked over to me.

"Man, that was some good ass."

He laughed and said, "See, that's what you get for judging people based on their age. Us older gentlemen know how to please. Remember, you will get old one day, too—even though forty-six isn't really old."

I rolled my eyes. *I'll worry about forty-six when I'm forty-six.*

He got out of the bed and went into the bathroom. He came back with a towel. I admired Pastor Williams' body. I hope I look that good when I'm forty-six. He reached into his wallet and pulled out three, one-hundred dollar bills. He walked over to the bed and handed them to me.

"Thanks," I said, standing up. I placed the money in my wallet. I finished wiping myself off, and then placed the towel on the floor. I put on my clothes. He went in the bathroom to clean up.

When he stepped out of the bathroom, he had on a pair of basketball shorts. Then, I heard it. He heard it, too. He looked at me. Panic spread across his face. Someone was home.

"Get in the closet," he whispered.

"Kendrick, where are you?" his wife, Dr. Jillian Williams said.

"Go!" he pushed me in there. He closed the bi-fold doors. I could see him leave the room. He closed the room door behind him.

"I'm right here!" I heard him yell. "I was in the bathroom."

"I left some papers on the table," she said. "Are you ok?"

"Yeah, I'm fine, why you ask?"

"You seem nervous," she paused. "Maybe the better word is disturbed."

Lord, please don't let this lady come in the room. This is not what I need.

"No, I'm fine," he said. "Just thinking about Sunday's message. Nothing major."

"Any way, I've gotta get back across town. I'll see you later. Are we still going out for dinner?"

"Yes," he said.

"Good, can't wait."

Moments later, I heard the door open and close.

Soon after, he was back in the room. Pastor Williams came to the closet and opened the door. He looked at me and said, "Wait around about ten minutes, then leave. I'm sorry; she wasn't supposed to come back home."

Sarcastically, I replied, "It's a good thing we were done, right?"

"Does your aunt know about your sexual orientation?"

"No." *At least it's never been publicly discussed.*

"Please, let's just keep this between us."

I looked at him and said, "If you ask me again not to tell someone, I'm gonna tell someone."

He said nothing else.

When those ten minutes were up, I checked my wallet to make sure I still had those three hundred dollars. Once the coast was clear, I headed out of his house and back to my car, which was parked at McDonald's.

The moment I sat down and turned on my car, my phone started to vibrate. I glanced at the name. It was my fuck buddy from Atlanta.

He has called me everyday since Friday, sometimes twice a day.

I pressed the talk button and said, "What's up?"

"Bryce, I've been trying to reach you all weekend."

"Yeah, I'm not in Atlanta...so we can't fuck."

"I'm not trying to fuck," he said.

"So, what the hell are you calling me for?" I

asked. *Fucking is the basis of our relationship. I'm not your friend. We're fuck buddies. Nothing more, nothing less.*

"I was calling to tell you," he paused.

"Calling to tell me what?"

He took a deep breath then cleared his throat. He said, "Well, long story short. I went in for a routine test and I found out I'm HIV-positive. It was confirmed on Thursday. I'm just letting you know so you can get yourself tested."

I felt like my heart stopped beating. All of my organs tightened up. My hands were shaking. I damn near shitted on myself.

"What did you just say to me?" I asked.

"I said, I just found out I'm positive and you need to get yourself tested. I don't know when I contracted it, but I just thought you should know...being we never used condoms."

I hung up the phone.

That nigga trippin'.

Then, I could hear his words—positive.

I shook my head in disbelief. No. No fucking way. No. I wasn't believing that. No.

HIV-positive? Hell naw. Get the fuck out of here with that bullshit...

~To Be Continued~

A Note from Jaxon

Thank you so much for reading my first novella, **Bad Religion**. I truly hope that you enjoyed this story. If you haven't, please check out my first trilogy, **Crimes of the Heart**. Also, be on the lookout for the first entry into my second trilogy, **Incidental Contact**. Thanks for all the love and support. You'll never know how much it means to me.

~Jaxon

About the Author

Known mostly as BnTasty by his online reader-base, Jaxon Grant, started his writing conquest in June 2008, on *Da Site,* which is a popular stories website for gay and bisexual men. With his initial publications, Jaxon captivated his audience and created a healthy following that urged him to move outside of the confines of those who flocked to *Da Site* to read his material. Now, after many years of growing and understanding his skills as a writer, he's finally taking the first steps to bring his work to a national audience.

In such a short span of time, Jaxon has added notch after notch in writing ten novels to date and currently he is completing the final volume for his sensational "Life of a College Bandsmen" series. Other titles that he has penned include: "Incidental Contact" and "What Webs We Weave." Jaxon plans to release all of his written work, title-by-title and will start with his "Crimes of the Heart" trilogy.

In this epoch, Jaxon has written with compelling thoughts that tackle the issues we face as American's, not just in the gay community. In his style, he uses the elements of drama, mystery, suspense, romance and tragedy to further the depth and scope of his work.

Jaxon was born and raised in Orlando, Florida. He attended Florida A&M University (FAMU) and majored in Social Science Education with a concentration in Political Science. While at FAMU, Jaxon was a member of the marching band, the word renown, FAMU Marching 100.

Please be sure to visit his website, www.jaxongrant.com, and sign up for his newsletter to receive important updates from Jaxon.